Vicious Lies

Ella Miles

PROLOGUE

ONCE UPON A TIME, I fell in love.

She was feisty, radiant, and reckless. She had nothing. She came from nothing. And unless she found a rich husband—it would take everything she had to pull herself out of poverty.

I wasn't rich.

I had less money than her.

I had no college degree.

No job prospects.

All I had was five dollars in my pocket and the clothes on my back.

None of that mattered.

Our love was enough.

We vowed to love each other forever.

We got married.

A baby followed.

I thought our life together was so happy.

I thought we could make our marriage last.

I thought...

I sigh.

I thought it was enough.

Turns out, you can't live on love.

You can't eat love.

Breathe love.

Live under a roof made of love.

You need money.

We tried to make more of ourselves. I went to a community college.

It wasn't enough.

She worked three jobs.

It wasn't enough.

Our baby deserved more.

We deserved more.

So we started hunting for a way out.

Hunting.

Hunting.

Hunting...

Until finally, we found a way out.

We had more money than we could have ever imagined.

More money than the suits who used to look down on us as we cleaned their homes.

More money than the executives who those suits reported to.

More money than the queen of England.

We thought we had it all. We thought we knew what came next.

But all that came next was defending what we had stolen.

Our love wasn't enough.

Fighting our enemies wore us down until we had no energy left. Until we had no desire to fight. Until our love dissolved into ash, and our hearts were torn apart.

Sometimes fairytales turn into nightmares.

Listen to my warning, child.

Don't search for it.

Don't seek the fairytale.

Don't seek the money like your mother and me.

Run, Liesel.

Hide.

Don't hunt.

Above everything else, don't ever tell anyone the truth—who you are or what you know.

"I don't understand," Liesel says.

I wish I could explain everything to her. I wish I had more time. I wish I could ensure she didn't make the same mistakes her mother and I did.

But there is no time.

And I can't make her decisions for her. I've failed as a father in more ways than one. All I can give her now is my advice and hope she makes the better choice, becomes the better person.

"It's all in here." I hand her an envelope.

She stares at it with big eyes as she begins to remove the letter from the envelope. "What is it?"

I put my hand over hers, stopping her.

"Later. Read it later, when you're alone. Then burn it. Forget about going after the money, the treasure. Lie to anyone who asks you about it."

I want to ask her to promise me, but I don't. That's too much to ask of her. Someday, she may choose to go after the treasure. She may think it's worth it. My only hope is that it is—for her.

Just please, God, don't let it destroy her like it did me.

"I have so many questions," she says.

"I know, and I wish we had more time."

"Is this goodbye?"

"It is, my sweet daughter. It is."

I lean forward and kiss her on the cheek. I wish I could apologize for all the shit I've put her through. There is no apology big enough to earn her forgiveness.

"Go," I say.

She takes a step out of the tiny house that she and her mother lived in for years when she was little. A house I lived in with them when she was first born, before I made the worst mistake of my life.

It takes everything inside me not to chase after her.

But I pulled myself out of her life a long time ago. I don't get to come back into her life now that she's an adult.

Liesel runs down the porch without glancing back.

She heads toward her car, and just before she reaches it, a boy approaches her. No, he's all man. Tall, dressed in dark clothes, but his hair light as the sun. The tenseness on his face and vein bulging on his forehead says he's pissed.

He stops her.

I want to protect her, save her.

I can't.

This is the life she was born into. I have no way to save her.

But my Liesel is more than capable of handling her own with this man. She yells back, pointing her finger at him as she storms around him to the driver's side of the car.

There is more yelling I can't make out, before she climbs into the car. He catches the door right before she slams it in his face.

One tense moment.

He slams the door.

She drives away.

The man stands there a moment—watching her.

And then he turns and looks right at me.

I glare back.

I see what's in his hand—a ripped piece of paper.

He must have torn part of the envelope when they were arguing.

I told Liesel to keep it a secret, but it's too late now. Now someone knows.

Now she has no choice but to lie.

Lie, Liesel—it's the only way to stay alive.

1

LIESEL

I WILL KILL YOU.

I read the words on the piece of paper in my hand. *Who puts death threats in the mail anymore?* It seems archaic and old-timey. There are so many better ways to send a threat: a phone call, a text message, an email.

An in-person act of violence really sends a message too, if you really have the balls.

Why write a letter?

Because he's a coward.

I consider tossing the letter in the trash and not taking the issue any further, forgetting that it even happened. But I didn't survive this long by tossing away idle threats.

I will kill you.

This isn't the first time someone has made a threat like this against me.

I will kill everyone you love.

Again, not new. I just thought I was passed this part of my life. I thought I was done living in this dangerous, vicious world. One where there are no winners—at least, I never win. I just survive.

I thought, just like letter writing, this part of my life was buried in the past.

I tap my painted red nails against my desk as I read the letter over two more times. Nothing hints at who the author is. There is no name scrolled across the bottom. Like I thought—*wuss*.

But that doesn't mean there aren't hints of who my enemy is. The way the letter is scribed tells me it's a man who wrote it. It was scribbled quickly with a pen almost out of ink on a piece of computer paper. This note was written last minute; it wasn't thought through.

And it didn't arrive in an envelope in the mail. It was stuffed loosely into the mailbox. I wouldn't be surprised if I found fingerprints.

Whoever sent this is an amateur, or at least, wants me to think he's an amateur.

I'm not an amateur. As much as I never thought I would know how to hold a gun, fire a weapon, hunt down men, rescue myself, I've never had a choice in the matter. My entire life I've lived in a cruel underworld of men who controlled everything. Men who had no right to own anything. Men who ruled with guns and darkness in their hearts, taking no prisoners. Taking what they wanted without concern of whom they hurt.

I used to be a princess in a world filled with dangerous men. I used to have friends who would protect me above everything else.

But things started slowly changing when my best friend, Enzo Black, fell in love. And then Zeke, my other protector, fell in love next. It's only a matter of time until Langston, the playboy of the group, falls in love.

I could call any one of them to take care of the man who sent this threat. Enzo, Zeke, or Langston all have the power and abilities to handle this man without lifting a finger.

That's what they do—kill dangerous men. They protect their family, which used to include me.

Until they failed me.

Until they fell in love.

Until I decided I didn't want to be a damsel in distress, waiting for a man to come and rescue me.

I saved myself.

I picked up every broken, shattered piece and put myself back together, painstakingly, piece by piece.

I'm whole now—even if the pieces don't fit together the same as they did before.

I'm a survivor—that's the term used to describe me. It's a term I hate, because I didn't just survive, I thrived. I fought back; I rescued myself. I'm a fucking knight in red high heels.

So while I could call my friends to save me and take care of this, I'm not going to. I haven't asked any one of them for help in years, and I'm not going to start now.

I lift my glass of scotch from my desk and swirl it around until the single ball of ice shifts in the glass, making a delicious rattling sound before I take a sip. I'm a woman in a man's world, but that doesn't mean I let the men rule me anymore. I won't give any man power over me—never again.

So that leaves me two choices. I can toss this letter in the trash and ignore it completely. There is a large chance whoever sent it will never grow enough balls to actually act on his threat. Or I go back into the world I never thought I would enter again.

A world of danger.

Cruelty.

Vows.

And lies.

A world that once consumed me. A world that turned me into the cold, heartless woman I've become. A world that took everything from me, yet gave me my power.

I thought I was done.

I thought this chapter of my life was over, buried.

I could leave it alone. For years, I've done everything I can to stay out of this life. To stay away from the evil that lurks in the night. Not because I'm afraid of the darkness hurting me. Not because I'm afraid that the man making the threat will actually succeed. Even if he did succeed, I'm not afraid of death.

No, I've stayed away from the darkness because I haven't wanted to become the villain I'm capable of being. Once the darkness surrounds me, I'll no longer be the princess. I'll become the evil queen. Once I let it in, there is no way to get it out. That's why I've put up walls around my heart, to keep the vile out, the wickedness I can become.

But why?

Why can't I turn into the evil queen?

My friends and family are gone. The only man in my life is more than capable of taking care of himself.

I shouldn't go back to this life.

I should crumple the letter up and toss it into the fireplace to burn.

I should forget the threat until it comes true.

But I feel the walls lowering around my heart. All the men in my life are able to stay safe and protect those they love, because they don't fight the worst parts of themselves.

Enzo is a controlling bastard, who rules his world by loving Kai.

Zeke protects those he loves no matter the cost it inflicts on himself.

And Langston hurts others to protect himself.

All three men have done more than survived; they've become kings. They've languished and destroyed their enemies. They've gained enough power that no man dares to make threats like this.

It's time I try their tactics.

I toss the rest of the scotch back into my throat before slamming the glass down on my desk with a sinful grin across my red-painted lips.

The evil that I locked in my heart is free. I'm going to use every bit of its power to take care of this threat myself, so no man or woman will ever threaten me again.

2

LANGSTON

I sit in the darkness.

I love the darkness, but I hate waiting.

I'm not a patient man. I leave that to my friend, Zeke.

But my excited anticipation keeps me seated in this pine smelling office. I glance around the room as my eyes quickly adjust to the lack of light.

The office is just what you'd expect from a rich prick with no taste. A large mahogany desk with an oversized office chair in the center of the main wall with the large oval-shaped window behind the chair. *Why wouldn't you want to look out the window when you work?* It's all for show.

The same with the large bookshelf filled with self-help books, classics, and business books. None look like they've ever been read.

There is a piece of art by Picasso finishing the room. But I know how big the man's bank account is. At best, it's a print; at worst, it's a complete knock off. A fake—just like this room, just like the man.

And then I spot the one thing in the room that looks like it has been used—the liquor cart.

I get up from my chair and pick up the bottle of scotch sitting on the cart and read the label. Highland Park Orcadian—an expensive bottle that's been aged a long time.

My eyebrows shoot up in pleasant surprise as I pour myself a glass. I walk back to my chair, my wait greatly improved now that I have an excellent glass of scotch to keep me company.

I take a sip and then spew the liquid everywhere as I lift the glass to eye level to get a better look. I sniff the liquid, and it smells as retched as it tastes. There is no way this is what's listed on the label.

I shake my head in disbelief as I set the glass down on the desk, making sure not to use a coaster so a ring will form on the ridiculously ugly desk. That's what he gets for trying to trick people into thinking they are drinking expensive liquor when I doubt he paid more than fifty bucks for that shit.

My patience is waning when I finally hear the front door open.

"This condo is amazing," the woman with him says, shouting too loudly and giving this condo way too much credit. The condo is a mass-produced, overpriced box.

"Not as amazing as you are," he says back.

I roll my eyes at the ridiculous line. But it's not going to take much to impress this woman. She's drunk and clearly impressed with what she perceives as his wealth. She doesn't know real wealth. She doesn't know that real money is passed through generations and earned by spilling blood of others.

This man is barely a millionaire. He doesn't have the billions that flow through the Black empire, my employer.

My plan was to wait in the office for him to come to me. He works in security. He should easily realize that his security system was turned off already when he came in. I purposefully scuffed my shoes along his rug until the corner lifted, and turned the frame crooked on the wall in the office hallway.

He should know I'm here within minutes.

If this were my home, I would know the second the alarm was turned off.

So I try to remain patient and let him come to me. But, again, I'm not patient. From the moaning and groaning floating down the hallway, it doesn't seem like he is paying attention to any of the clues I left for him.

I open the office door and walk down the hallway, not hiding the sound of my footsteps. I walk toward the living room where I find them making out on the couch like horny teenagers. The kisses are sloppy, and from the way he's manhandling the poor woman, there is no way she's going to get off tonight from him.

I step into the light, but he still doesn't notice me. However, the woman's eyes shoot up to me. She shrieks out of surprise, but then her eyes are running up my body appreciatively. She'd rather I be fucking her than the schmuck she's straddling.

"Get up," I say calmly and firmly, keeping the anger I feel out of my voice.

The woman scampers off, listening obediently. The man only slowly turns his head.

"I said. Get. Up."

He swallows, and I know the options he's considering in his head. But he's an amateur, and I'm a skilled assassin.

He reaches for his gun, but I grab it, empty the magazine, and toss it to the floor.

His eyes grow big, his pupils dilate, his pulse beats rapidly in his throat as the fear spreads. He's defenseless. He has nothing to match my skill. Basically, he's my bitch, and he knows it.

His bottom lip trembles as he considers his next words,

but none come out. I'm surprised the man hasn't pissed himself yet.

"Who are you?" the woman asks, licking her bottom lip. Apparently, I'm not scary enough to her. She thinks she can seduce me with her good looks. But she's as fake as this apartment—her curves don't come naturally. Neither does her bleach blonde hair or her pointed fingernails.

I turn my attention to her. My heated gaze ponders all the ways I could fuck her. She might be good in bed, but there are a million reasons I won't fuck her. The main one being that I'm in love with another woman.

"Go to the bedroom," I say to her.

Her smile curves up, revealing her wine-stained teeth and lips. Her breath catches as I stare at her before she obediently walks toward the bedroom.

With her gone, I can focus on my main task.

"What—what do you want?" the man asks, his voice trembling as he speaks. He knows exactly what I want.

I take my time strolling around the sofa between us as I casually sit in the single chair facing him, acting like I'm about to negotiate with him. There is no way that's going to happen, though. I'm in control, not him, and I know exactly how his story ends.

"I—I have money. You can have whatever you want."

"I don't want your money."

I adjust my watch, completely bored with this conversation, this task, this world.

I was hired to kill this man. For months now, I've been taking odd jobs like this to soothe my killer instinct. To get a little thrill, a little bit of danger in my life. Something I used to get working for Enzo Black, but the Black empire has grown so big, so powerful that no one dares to stand up to him. No one has threatened them in months. The job has become boring and unsatisfying.

But I'm finding that these jobs, hunting and killing killers, is even less exciting.

"Mr. Reynolds, thank you for helping me realize something," I say, standing like I'm about to end a business meeting.

His eyes fill with hope, and I can see the relief filled smile stretch over his lips.

"What's that?"

I crack my neck casually. His life means nothing to me. This is what I do. I hunt, I protect, I kill.

I pull out my gun and aim it at his heart.

"I've realized that you are going to be my last job." And then I squeeze the trigger, watching him drop to a puddle of blood on the floor as his heart squirts out blood.

I walk out the door before his date for the night comes out and realizes what happened. I'm not worried that she's going to report me to the police. I don't care that my prints are all over the condo. The police are no threat to me.

I take the elevator down, walk out to my motorcycle and start it up. This is definitely my last job. I don't need the money, I only do it for the thrill, and the thrill is gone.

My phone buzzes, most likely Adrian, the man who got me this job. I pull it out to answer him when I see the message come through. I'm already getting sent another job because I'm the best hitman. That's all this town sees me as.

They don't know that killing people doesn't even touch the depths of my capabilities.

They don't know exactly how evil my heart is.

They don't know what I've done, what I'm about to do.

I consider just deleting the message without reading it, but the way it starts catches my attention.

Hitman Needed.

. . .

I don't need you to find the man who made a death threat. I'll find him.

I don't need you to kidnap him. I can do that too.

I don't even need you to actually kill him.

All I need you to do is say that you killed him if the need should arise. Just be there so I can say I didn't kill him.

You have to have a record. And you have to have killed before.

I'll pay one hundred thousand.

—Huntress

I read the message three times before I accept that I'm not dreaming. This is my chance for payback, for redemption, for revenge.

Huntress.

It's been years since I've called her huntress. I don't think I've called her that since we were teenagers. And yet, she's using it here to hide her identity.

Or she's calling out to me? Hoping I'll be the one to answer her ad?

Not likely, since she hates my guts.

But this is too good an opportunity to pass up.

I kick my foot down, starting up my motorcycle as I text back: Accepted.

Then I slip the phone into my pocket, instead of deleting the message like I should. I keep it, knowing I'll want to reread the message over and over again as a plan forms in my head.

I shouldn't have accepted. I should stay far away from my

huntress. She's destroyed me before, and there is a good chance she'll do it again.

But this time, things are different. This time, I won't give her my heart. This time, I plan on being the one who wins.

3

LIESEL

ONLY ONE MAN responded to my message—*unusual*.

As shocking as it may seem to some people, this isn't my first time hiring a hitman. And only getting one response isn't typical, not in a town like this.

We are supposed to meet for coffee in SoHo. It's a trendy third-wave coffee shop that is almost always standing room only, so plenty of people to ensure neither of us is in any danger.

I'm not worried about being in any danger regardless. We could be meeting in a back alley alone, and I still wouldn't be afraid to meet him, whoever he is.

Fear is something that I no longer feel. My fear was taken from me years ago.

We are supposed to meet at ten o'clock.

I purposefully show up ten minutes late. I don't like to wait; I'm not a patient woman. And if he's not willing to wait ten minutes, then he's not the man for the job.

My heels click on the tile floor as I walk to order my drink—a coffee, black. I have no need for extra calories in

21

the form of sugar or milk. Only once I have my coffee in hand do I turn to look for the man I'm meeting.

We didn't exchange any details about each other. And it's not like one of us is holding a single rose or something stupid like that from the movies.

I'm dressed in a slim navy blue dress and heels. I look like any other woman headed to work in the city. He's not going to be able to find me. I'm going to have to be the one to find him.

I walk confidently through the throng of people gathered around the too-small tables. Most people are chatting in a group—those I can rule out. There are a few on their laptops —I rule them out as well. I don't see a single person on their own.

I sigh as I sip my coffee. I'll walk through the room one more time, and if I don't find him, I'll have to put out a new call for a hitman. I'm not going to deal with a man being late.

Suddenly, goosebumps form down my arms, the hairs on the back of my neck stand up, and all of the air squeezes from my lungs. I don't have to turn around to know who is standing behind me.

This can't be a coincidence. *I haven't seen him in seven, or is it eight months?* He doesn't live here. He saw my call for a hitman, and he answered it. And I have no doubt he knew exactly who he was answering. I used the nickname that only he calls me.

"Huntress," Langston says, sending shivers racing through my body.

I try not to react. Only Langston has the ability to turn my body on end. To make me feel things I didn't know I was capable of feeling. And not all of those feelings are good.

"Killer," I say in a raspy voice, using the nickname I gave for him when we were kids, after I learned that he had killed a deer hunting. If I had only known then that he kills a lot more than deer…

The flame that burns intensifies as we let it simmer between us. We both relish the feeling, even though we will never do a thing about it. An electric energy between two people doesn't mean that we belong together. In fact, I think it means we should stay as far away from each other as possible. If we light a match near our smoldering fire, we will burn the entire world to the ground.

I turn around, hoping that I'm in complete control. That I look confident, poised, and completely unaffected. But when I look at Langston, it's not what I expect. He's wearing a suit. He never wears a suit.

It fits him well, which means he owns it and isn't renting it. It's a dark gray color with a white shirt opened at the collar, exposing his delicious sculpted chest. It also hides the muscles and scars underneath, which tell the story of the dangerous life Langston leads.

He doesn't look like a gangster, a devil, a killer. Instead, he looks like a businessman meeting a client for coffee.

"This is a new look for you," I say, my eyes purposefully trailing down his suit instead of staring at the harsh edges of his jaw and blue depths of his eyes that I'll get lost in if I stare too long.

"This is the same look for you," he says. His voice gives nothing away, but it's meant to be a compliment. He's always liked the way I look—neat, tidy, polished with just a hint of womanly curves.

"Shall we sit, or should we just agree this isn't going to work and go on with our separate lives?" I ask, lifting my cup to my lips, daring him to be the one to decide if he wants to take this meeting further. I don't want him to go, and I know he won't. He wouldn't have come all the way from Miami to meet me in New York City for coffee if he wasn't going to stay and talk to me.

The edge of his lip lifts, reminding me of the playful boy I used to know as a kid before the world darkened him and turned him into a monster that I barely even recognize. And then he walks past me. For a moment, I think he's leaving, but he walks to a small table in the corner where a couple of college-aged boys are laughing with two empty coffee cups.

"Time to leave, boys," Langston says, his voice low and deep, full of a harsh threat if they stay.

I don't have to be a fortune teller to know the boys will get up without protest. I know the look that Langston is giving them, I've heard the voice. No one denies him when he uses it. His voice alone holds that kind of power, which makes it all the more shocking that he doesn't use it to rule his own empire. Instead, he follows others' orders.

Langston pulls out a chair for me to sit.

I won't sit in it. He already knows this, which is why he gives me a smug knowing smile when I sit in the opposite chair. He takes his seat as well, and we both place our cups of coffee on the table.

"So, my little huntress is going to finally make a kill?" Langston asks.

"I guess that means we aren't going to small talk first." I cross my legs, purposefully pushing the hem on my dress higher up my thigh.

Langston's eyes flick down to my legs before meeting my gaze again. "I'd rather get right to the point than play games with you."

I smile. "We never play games with each other, killer. We just lie."

The disappointed frown Langston gives me affects me more than I want to admit.

"Yes, I plan on killing someone," I finally say.

"Who?"

"Does it matter?"

Langston shrugs. "Not really, but it's not like you to actually kill a man. You hunt them down, you track them, but you never do the killing. Never get your pretty little hands dirty."

"No, that's your job."

"So did you change your mind? Am I the one who is going to do the killing?"

I shake my head. "This one's mine."

His eyes narrow into tight slits as he stares deep into mine. There was a time where we could both read each other with one look. That time has long passed. He has no idea what's going on behind my hazel eyes. No idea what I'm hiding beneath the mask of makeup, curled blonde hair, and tight dress.

"Why?" he asks when he can't find the answer on his own.

I lift my coffee to my lips, avoiding giving him an answer.

"Tell me the truth. Why did you come when you knew it was me who sought a killer?" I ask.

"Now, why would I do that? We never tell each other the truth," Langston says, his voice angry and sultry as he throws my words back at me. It might be the only truth we ever tell each other.

I toss my hair over my shoulder. "This was a mistake. I'll find someone else."

Langston leans back in his chair. If I got up and ran out, I know he wouldn't chase me.

We never chase.

We don't play games.

We just lie. And lie and lie.

It's the only thing I can count on when it comes to us.

"No, you won't," Langston says.

I frown, my eyes flitting back and forth over his, trying to figure out the hidden meaning.

"I will. I don't need you."

"It's me or no one." His blue eyes shine brightly. He knows he has me cornered. And he's about to go in for the kill.

"I'll make sure that every man knows that you're mine. That you are tied to the Black name."

I grip my coffee cup tighter but don't show any other outward signs of my anger. "Always using the Black name instead of your own."

"The Black name is my own."

I run my tongue over my teeth, drawing his attention to my mouth. "Just another lie. You can pretend that it doesn't matter that you aren't Enzo's brother by blood, but it matters. He has a real brother now. He has another best friend. You are nothing but a disposable soldier to him."

I stand to get up. I don't need a hitman anyway. I can kill the man myself. And I can find a way to ensure that no one ties me to the crime.

Langston catches my wrist, though, before I'm even fully out of my chair. I'd forgotten how quick his reflexes are.

"When?" he asks, not letting me have any control. Just one of the many reasons why we will never work.

I inhale a deep breath, taking my time. I may not be able to deny him, but I can prolong my answer. It's a mistake, though, because all I smell is his husky scent. It fills my nostrils, and it's going to linger there all day. Every time I take a breath in, I'll breathe in him—a burning reminder of a man I wish I could get rid of forever.

"Saturday night." I don't give him any more specific details. I don't have to tell him what time or where. I know he'll find me. *He always finds me.*

He nods.

I think he's finally going to release me, but his hand is still wrapped around my wrist.

"We still need to discuss payment," he says.

"$100K. I told you how much in the ad."

He shakes his head. "I don't want your money."

"That's the only way I'll pay you."

His jaw tightens, and I chance a glance at his eyes. He doesn't have to tell me with words how I will pay him back. I know. I know what he wants from me. The same thing most men want from me.

But it's the one thing I'll never give him.

4

LANGSTON

LIESEL RAN from the only family she's ever known. She did it years ago to start a new life. To get a fresh start. To stay away from what she deemed evil and brought up too many painful memories for her.

I understood at the time why she ran.

I know why she's disappointed in me.

I know why she's been gone all this time.

She's been running from her past. But it seems her past has caught up with her.

For a while, she lived in the middle of nowhere. She was hidden. *Safe.*

But that isn't the life for Liesel. She likes to be near people; she likes to matter. So she moved back to the city and started up her life again as a lawyer. She bought a high-rise condo. She became the powerful woman she once was. She thought she could hide in plain sight, but there is no hiding from our world.

I know—I've tried. Once you are in this world, you are in. There is no quitting. You can try to outrun it, but eventually, the darkness from your history catches up to you.

Liesel wants to hunt and kill a man.

She's always been a hunter, but never a killer. That was always where she drew the line. It's just another reason she hates me.

I don't only kill for self-protection; I kill because I enjoy it.

She left the coffee shop without telling me who or why. But I have time.

Saturday, she said. Today is Tuesday. I have four days until I see her again. Four days to figure out the truth she's hiding. The lies she spoke.

We never tell each other the truth. We can't.

It started as games when we were children. But then I stole half of a secret that I had no right to. She has half of the truth; I have the other half. Both of us will lie forever to keep our secrets.

My heart pounds in the cage that is my ribs as I think about seeing her again in person instead of watching her from the shadows or on a shitty security camera.

She's the same—exquisite beauty, full of all the confidence in the world. But that's her outward appearance. On the inside, she's a broken bird hiding beneath giant wings. She hasn't ever dealt with her past so she can never really live her future. She's living a half-life, one where she doesn't fully exist.

You could say the same thing about me.

For now, though, I have a new obsession. One I will enjoy immensely. I get to watch, study, and learn everything I can about Liesel.

She knows that's what I'm doing. It's why she didn't tell me all the details about where or even exactly when to meet her. She knows I can figure it out. And I haven't had such a thrill surge through me in months.

The next four days, I become mesmerized by her. I have

an excuse to watch her more closely than I ever have before. She may think she was out of my life, but I've been keeping tabs on her. It's the most patient I've ever been, waiting for the moment she returned to my life. This wasn't the way I expected her to return, but I welcome it all the same.

I tapped into the security feed in her condo and spent most of my nights watching her. Unfortunately, there are only cameras in the main living portion, so the most I get to see of her is when she walks through the living room and then out the door in the morning. She doesn't even make a cup of coffee in her kitchen when she wakes up. She sticks to her bedroom. I don't know if it's her usual routine or if she knows I'm watching and is purposefully making it harder for me to see her.

But once outside her condo, she can't hide.

I follow her in her cab.

I watch her strut like a true New York woman in her high heels and tight dresses as she enters her office building every day with her name scrawled across the nameplate leading to the top floor of a sky-rise. She's the queen of her own domain.

The security in her office building has cameras every-where. Watching her give orders in the boardroom to her team, give advice in a controlling yet flirtatious way to her clients, and then answer calls like a boss has me growing hard. Especially when she crosses her legs when she's alone in her office and lets her dress inch higher up her thigh until it's no longer professional. She holds a pen to her lips and sucks on the end, her long lashes fluttering up to the corner of her office every once in a while where the security camera sits.

My little huntress, drawing me in as she acts like a seductive minx, putting on a show just for me. And what a show it is. I could spend the rest of my life watching her.

But then I remember the truth. I remember who she is. What she's done.

You think you want to kill, my huntress? You have no idea how. You have no idea what killing will do to you. And what need do you have to kill when you can seduce and draw a man in with one flick of your tongue across your bottom lip, one bat of your eyelashes, one raspy word from your voice? Men spend their entire lives looking for a woman like you.

I've had you this entire time.

Men are stupid; they don't realize the thing they are drawn to is all a lie.

Liesel gets up from her desk and grabs her purse.

I frown as I look at the time. Four-thirty, way too early for her to be done with work for the day. Liesel is a workaholic. She usually isn't done for the day until seven or eight. And then even after work is over, she usually meets a client for dinner. And I suspect she still goes over files in her bedroom at night. She's never done working.

Where are you going, huntress?

It's Friday, my last day to figure out where to meet her and who she wants to kill. I haven't spent much time on the man she wants to hunt and kill. I've been much too focused on watching her.

Anyway, I could find the man in twenty minutes or less after I put some effort in, which I will tonight. For now, I need to know where she is going. I need to know everything about her.

Her cab stops in front of another shiny, high-rise building. My guess is that she's meeting another client at their office instead of her own.

I park my car illegally on the side of the road and watch her from the driver's seat. She doesn't go into the building immediately. Instead, she pulls out her phone and talks on it for a few minutes as she paces back and forth.

A man comes out in a suit—the client she's meeting.

I study him closer as he approaches her and then pulls her into an aggressively tight hug. He's at least a decade older than her, his hair has speckles of gray in it, and he has more wrinkles around the eyes than any man our age.

The hairs on my arms stand up, and in my gut, I know this man isn't a client.

Who is he?

His vile hand slips down from around her lower back, gripping her ass. His other hand tips her head back as his thumb strokes her carotid, like if she makes one wrong move, he'll apply just the right amount of pressure to kill her and make it look like an accident. It's a threatening move I've made too many times myself.

This is the man she is hunting.

This is the man she plans on killing tomorrow.

My gorgeous huntress, what trouble did you get into? What did he do to you to make you change your mind about killing men?

He had to have done more than just grope her inappropriately. Unfortunately, that's something that she is used to. Men can't control themselves around her—they turn into disgusting, rotten pigs who touch without asking.

Liesel knows how to handle men like that. I taught her in the fifth grade how to knee a man in the balls.

So I watch with a smirk, waiting for the moment when she'll bring this asshole to his knees.

Her face tilts up with a smug smile. This is it—the moment she makes him pay for touching her without her permission.

She leans forward, closing the space between them as he plants a firm kiss on her lips.

I jump out of my car without thinking. My legs start moving toward them. *He has no right to touch her!* She didn't ask him to touch her. She didn't welcome his kiss. She didn't—

The kiss ends, and I stop in my tracks as I watch her smile up at the man with more brightness than I knew existed in Liesel.

This man made her smile with a kiss.

That's.

Not.

Possible.

Liesel doesn't smile, not like that. She prowls and smirks and flashes seductive grins. But she doesn't smile from true joy and happiness.

And yet, that's exactly what she's doing. She's smiling up at a man a decade older.

Her hand is slipping into his, their fingers intertwining like they've done this a million times.

Her purse falls down her shoulder, and he takes it off and loops it over his shoulder, making her laugh.

She's laughing.

I'm not close enough to hear it, but I'm close enough to see the sparks flying from her face.

Liesel is happy.

I never thought I'd see the day.

This isn't the man she plans on killing tomorrow.

But he's the man I want to kill for touching what's mine.

5

LIESEL

I felt Langston all week.

He was watching me every second of every day. I doubt he slept a minute all week.

Langston hasn't changed at all. I know him better than anyone else.

I avoided the security cameras in my home that I know he tapped into. I avoided most of my usual evening routine.

The only time I put a show on for him was at the office. I drew him in like a hunter draws in prey. I just haven't decided when or how I'm going to strike against him. At least not yet.

For now, I have more important matters to attend to. I have to kill the man who threatened me and my family.

I have to stop thinking about Langston. It's impossible, though, since I feel him everywhere now. It's a strange, yet familiar feeling. One that sends goosebumps up my spine at the most inconvenient times.

But Langston will serve his purpose. He'll take the fall if or when the time comes for my blackmailer's death. And then he will get out of my life once again, gone in the night just like before. And I can go back to the life I've chosen.

I slip on my white gloves as Waylon enters my bathroom. He hasn't been sleeping over the last couple of nights since I've wanted to throw Langston off and not give him any information about my life.

But I know he saw us kiss yesterday afternoon. I felt Langston's heated, angry stare. He wasn't happy with that kiss.

Well, too bad. I haven't been happy with Langston my entire life.

"You ready, my love?" Waylon asks, as he leans against the doorframe, watching me. His eyes drag down my body, taking every inch of me in, sending butterflies fluttering through my stomach and up my chest.

Waylon's effect on me is different than any other man I've ever met. It's more intense. More passionate. Just more.

It took me months to decide if that was a good thing or a bad thing. I still haven't decided, and we've been together for over a year. I don't think I ever will.

But it's a feeling. There was once a time that I didn't think I could ever feel. So I welcome feeling anything at all, even if it isn't exactly pleasant.

I meet his eyes in the mirror. He's wearing a tux that makes him look rugged and sophisticated. It's black, like his hair, lightly peppered with gray. When we first met, he used to color it, but I find the fact that he's older, more mature, and understands the world more than I do, comforting. And I admit, a bit sexy. So he stopped—for me.

His jaw is clean-shaven, showing off its squareness. His eyes are dark with a few lines in the corner that show the depths of his knowledge and worldly experience.

Even though he's leaning against the wall, his posture is

impeccable. He never falters on that. He always stands tall and proud—that's what I love most about him.

We are the same, him and I—we've been handed shitty cards, but we rose above it all. In our own way, we've found our power. And now together, we will rule this city—queen and king.

"Yes," I say, standing from my makeup chair and letting him see the full effect of my hair, makeup, and dress all at once.

Waylon's smile grows from ear to ear. "You're perfect, my beautiful one."

I force myself to smile. I hate compliments, but I should accept one from Waylon.

He holds out his arm, and I take it. He leads me to the waiting limo to take us to a ball where we will wine and dine all night, showing the city what true royalty looks like.

The ballroom is grand and sparkling as we enter. Tonight's facade is a fundraiser to feed the hungry in the city, but it's really an excuse for all the wealthy to dress up, network, and show off. They gain more power by making small threats and puffing out their chests to show that they should be the ones in control. That's what all these men and women are doing. They don't know that they've already lost. Waylon and I have already won.

Or maybe they do. Because all eyes in the room are on us from the second we enter. Everyone tries to jockey for our attention. Everyone murmurs, speaking in hushed tones about us.

I grin. Tomorrow my cheeks are going to hurt from all the smiling, but I'll keep doing it if it gains me more power.

"I hear you are running for governor," one of the men says.

"So word has gotten out already," Waylon laughs it off.

I flick Waylon a knowing look. We were the ones who

leaked the news. Waylon is running for governor today. Tomorrow it could be the presidency.

He wants power, real power, legal power—unlike some people I know.

That's what draws me to him.

Langston Pearce.

He's hidden from my view among a group of men chatting together. All I can see is a single eye peeking out from between two people. An eye watching me with unsettling dominance.

I wobble on my heels as my knees weaken from the power of his gaze.

Waylon may make me feel things I've never felt before, but Langston is the only man who can turn my knees weak, my heart still, and my world on its head.

Both men have a strong effect on me. Both men make me wish I'd never met them, because being with them means giving up some of my absolute control.

Neither man will let me have complete control. They want it for themselves.

My life would have been the same with Langston as it is with Waylon—a constant battle of wills. The difference is Waylon makes me stronger, while Langston makes me weaker. And I won't accept weakness.

I draw my eyes away as I hold onto my champagne glass, blocking my face from Langston's view.

The group mingling with us laughs at something Waylon says, and I laugh along with them. I could play my role in my sleep—the role of a trophy wife, clinging to Waylon's arm. And yet, I won't cling. I'm not here because of Waylon. I'm here on my own. I made it on my own. I don't need any man, Waylon knows it. He can't control me. It's why he knows that if I touch his arm, it's not because I need him to lean on. It's because I'm playing the part.

Still, when I'm drawn back into the conversation, I'm no longer really here. Instead, I'm focused on the feeling of Langston's eyes lingering over me, heating me from head to toe with just his hungry gaze.

From the outside, I ignore his stare. But Langston's wreaking havoc on my insides—my gut is twisted, my heart is fluttering, my breath is shallow, practically panting to breathe him in.

But then I see Fitz—the other man I'm here for. The man I've hunted down and traced to the threatening letter I was sent—a man I plan on killing.

"Excuse me, gentlemen," I say with a seductive smile before I kiss Waylon on the cheek and whisper into his ear that I'll be back soon.

He nods solemnly before turning back to entertaining the group around us. He doesn't ask where I'm going. He lets me be as independent as I want, even if he disagrees with me.

I spot Fitz, my target, as I strut through the ballroom. I know I have several eyes on me, but I only feel Langston's. I don't let myself look at him. I know where I stand with Langston. I know that although we will never be together, never even be friends, he will follow me. So I focus on my target.

A waiter walks over to the group he's standing in, leaning in to offer more champagne. And I take my chance.

I step right into the center of the five man group. All eyes and voices fall, as they all concentrate on keeping their boners from making an appearance as they drool over my body covered in lace and black fabric. My ass and legs look great beneath the slit in the dress, but my boobs are the real show as the dress cuts down in a low V, showing off most of my breasts.

Men are so easy to manipulate when you have a body like mine.

I set my empty glass on the tray, leaning across Fitz's face as I do. I stand almost a foot taller than him in my heels. Then I take another glass of champagne from the tray.

"Meet me on the balcony," I whisper into his ear before I turn and walk away toward the balcony. I know that he's following me without having to turn and look. In fact, I know that two men are following me.

The air is warm as I stand on the balcony a dozen floors up, looking out at the twinkling lights of the city. Anywhere else, a balcony like this might seem romantic. But here in New York City, the city that never sleeps, all you hear is the honk of horns and the bustle of people. You breathe in the heavy haze in the air. This sight, the energy here, makes me never want to leave.

"You found me," I say when I hear Fitz's heavy footsteps. He would make a terrible assassin, which is one of the reasons I was able to find him so easily. He's used to dealing with much less skilled people. He didn't know he was dealing with a survivor. He doesn't know that I more than survive—I thrive. And I won't let a nameless suit like him threaten my life. I've survived much worse men. This man is nothing. Soon, he'll truly be a nothing.

"When a beautiful woman tells you to meet her, you meet her."

I hold my champagne glass up as I turn and lay eyes on him, reading him like a book. He knows exactly who I am. He knows that I know who he is. He has a bulge in the side of his pants, where I know he keeps his weapon. He thinks I'm weak, that he can just pull the gun out, and I'll be on my knees begging for my life, willing to do whatever he wants.

Not likely.

I'd rather die.

"Your first lie, Mr. Fitz Nash." I sip the too sweet champagne.

He puts his hands in his pockets, close to the gun, but not quite touching it as he takes a couple of steps toward me.

"I don't lie."

He stops and leans against the cement railing next to me.

I let my eyelashes bat up at him, drawing him in as I lick my bottom lip. He leans closer, thinking I'm going to kiss him. I'll do a lot to hunt a man. I'll play my part, but I'll never kiss or fuck a man I don't want to, just to get what I want. That's where I draw the line.

There will be no kiss.

"No, you're just a blackmailing bastard who thinks he can threaten me and my family for easy money."

His eyes blink in shock, and he reaches for his gun. But I'm faster.

I smash my champagne glass hard against his forehead. He palms the large gash while I take the moment to casually grab his gun.

It takes the bastard a few minutes to realize what's happening; he's so focused on the blood pouring down the front of his face, dripping into his eyes, spilling onto his lips and tux. He doesn't realize I'm aiming a gun at his heart.

Slowly, he raises his hands.

"You're not going to kill me."

I remove the safety. "Why do people keep saying that?"

"Because it's true. You don't have to kill me. I'll leave you and your family alone."

"Why? Why did you target us? Was it just about the money, or was it more?" *Please, don't say it was about the blasted letter my father gave me before he disappeared from my life.*

"I knew you two had money. I thought with your family's political ambitions that you would just pay and move on. I never intended to harm you."

He lowers his hands.

I don't know why I'm letting him talk. This is all information I can get on my own. And I suspect he isn't telling the truth. *Just shoot him.*

"Are you working alone?" I ask, instead.

He smirks, thinking I'm weak. It's exactly what I need to be able to pull the trigger.

I squeeze.

Unfortunately, he moves just in time, and I only graze his arm. His eyes grow wide, and the air changes as he realizes I truly do intend to kill him. And there is no one to save him.

The city is too loud for anyone to put a thought to the occasional gunshot. And everyone in the party is already occupied. They don't care about the outside world.

"Goodbye, Fitz." I squeeze the trigger, but a loud movement to my side makes me turn.

Langston.

I frown as I realize what he's done. The gun is battled out of my hand. Fitz holds the gun to my head.

I'm the hunter who never kills.

Because Langston is the killer.

That much will never change.

6

LANGSTON

LIESEL WAS ACTUALLY GOING to kill this shithead.

She *would* have killed him.

I *couldn't* let her kill—not a low life like him. When she kills, it needs to be worth it. Her first kill will stay with her forever, as will each kill after that. I don't want her thinking about this bastard one second longer than she has to.

Liesel's fuming at me as Fitz grips her around the neck with one arm and holds the gun at her temple. She's not scared; she doesn't fear for her life. She knows that I won't let anyone hurt her, but her red cheeks, teeth biting down on her lip, and daggers for eyes let me know how pissed she is.

"You couldn't let me have him," she spits out as she pulls from Fitz's grasp, almost getting away on her own without my help.

I stand still as a statue, hoping that if I let her think about this a minute, she'll calm down. As long as she's in Fitz's hold, she has time to realize she shouldn't be fighting me. I already know how she'll feel in my arms.

As much as I yearn for that, and hate to see her in another man's, I can't have what I want. I never get what I want.

Yet, it won't stop me from demanding it, from eventually getting it. I'm tired of being patient when it comes to Liesel. Our story has lingered on for far too long. It's time to end it.

"You're the huntress," I say.

She shakes her head, her anger pulsing off her in waves. "You're the killer."

Fitz's eyes narrow as he takes me in, trying to understand who I am and what I'm doing here. Unlike Liesel, though, I won't be asking any questions.

"Don't take a step forward, or I'll kill her," Fitz says.

I smirk. *If he killed her, it would make my life a lot easier.*

Liesel notices my smirk, and her glare intensifies, as if to say, *I'll kill you and haunt you from the grave if you let me die.*

I give one look to Liesel, letting her read my thoughts like we used to be able to do as kids. She slams her elbow into Fitz's groin.

It's enough to get him to release her.

I take slow steps forward as Fitz hunches over in pain. I grab his gun that he so carelessly let Liesel take from him. He almost let her kill him. I pocket it from Liesel, and then I snap his neck. His body falls to the ground in one crumple.

Liesel gasps. Even though she's seen death hundreds of times. Even though she's seen me kill—it still takes her breath away every time.

After a moment, she composes herself and stares at me with such a harshness in her eyes as she folds her arms across her chest.

"I knew I should have found someone else," Liesel says.

I don't answer her. *She should have found someone else.* But she found me. She always finds me. That's why our lives keep intertwining.

I step closer to her. I expect her to slap me. To try and knee me in the balls. For her to try and steal my gun.

She does none of those things. She just lets me get close to her.

"If you need to kill someone, you call me. You don't do it yourself," I growl my command at her.

She scoffs. "Since when do I take orders from you?"

I grab her hips and jerk her to me until her chest is flush against mine.

"Never." *But you will soon, my huntress. You will soon. You won't have a choice.*

The music carries from the ballroom, making me want to dance now that Liesel is in my arms. So that's what I do. I sink my fingers into her lush hips, and we sway together.

It's wrong for so many reasons.

There is a dead man on the floor next to us.

We aren't together.

We will never be together.

She's with Waylon.

And I'm—well, my situation is complicated.

And yet, I can't not touch her. I can't not have her. It's always been this way with us. Even when she was in love with my best friend. Even when she finally set her eyes on me, we both knew that we could never be.

We just never speak the reasons out loud. The reasons would all be lies anyway. That's the one thing we share—lies.

We both grew up lying to survive, and it's stayed with us.

"What are you doing with Waylon Brown?" I ask.

She tilts her head as she looks up at me, her long throat revealed to me, and if I dip my head lower, I can see her glorious tits staring up at me. But it's her pulse in her neck that has my attention. I can see how fast her heart is racing.

Liesel wasn't scared of the man who held a gun to her head. She's scared of me. She knows I'm no longer on her side—and she knows I'm far more dangerous than Fitz was. I could harm her, kill her.

"He's rich and good looking, why wouldn't I be with him?" she answers back, tilting her head all the way back as I dip her over the ledge, knowing the danger makes her conflicted between desire and terrified. It also gives me the view of her elated face, and of course, I take the moment to run both my hand and eyes down the front of her dress. Her skin melts like hot silk beneath my fingers.

"Liar. You don't care about money. Or good looks."

I pull her back up, whipping her hard into my body. The movement takes her breath away.

"Power then?" she says it like a question.

I shake my head. *That's a lie too.* Everything the woman says is a lie. I haven't figured out what she's doing with that man yet, but I will.

I just have to read between the lines, do some investigating. There is always a reason with Liesel, and it's never the obvious. She would never let herself fall in love. Even though she doesn't supply love as an answer, I know that's not why she's with him.

"I didn't think you owned a tux," she says, her eyes suffocating my body with her stare.

"I don't."

She rolls her eyes, calling out my lie, before her eyes flick to the dead man on the floor, and suddenly she's sober.

"Why did you want him dead?" I ask, even though I already know the answer. I found the security video of her reading the blackmail, the threat against her family.

"Stop asking questions you already know the answer to."

She pushes away until she's no longer in my arms.

My arms hang at my side like dead weights, no longer having a purpose.

"I'll wire you the money I owe," she says, still staring at Fitz.

"I already told you, I don't want your money."

Liesel finally looks at me, her face unreadable. But I know she's scheming, trying to come up with a way to hurt me.

Just like I'm conniving ways to hurt her.

"You'll take care of the body?" she asks, already knowing I will. This isn't the first time I've killed a man. I work in security for the Black family, a crime family who rules the seas. I've disposed of plenty of bodies and killed more times than most people make new acquaintances.

I walk over to the body. There's a reason I didn't shoot him. I don't want to haul a body down the stairs.

"Stand back," I order.

For once, Liesel listens as I squat down to stare at the bastard. I should be thanking him. He gave me a reason to be in Liesel's life again.

Then I heave him up over the railing and watch as his body falls down the twelve stories and hits the sidewalk below.

There is a soft screech that reaches our ears from up here.

People will believe it was a suicide. I'll take care of the security cameras so no one knows we were up here with him.

Even if the police don't believe it, they won't trace his death to us. And if they found out someone in the Black family was involved, they wouldn't care. They know they have no power against us. We rule wherever we go.

I grab Liesel's arm—she trembles at my touch, and then I lead her back inside, off the balcony. Just because I can convince the police of anything doesn't mean I want to deal with them.

Liesel doesn't comment on how I decided to deal with the body. She may not have spent her life killing, but she's watched me kill. She's watched Enzo and Zeke. She's seen as much death as I have. She's felt as much loss.

She's just as broken and fucked up as I am.

I stop us in the hallway, and I cage her in, putting my arms on either side of her head. She doesn't act like she's trapped, though.

That's because she's not. My tricks don't work on her, just like hers don't work on me.

"We're done then. I won't see you again for six months or more. And when we both go to our friends' birthday parties for their kids, we won't speak to each other. Yes?" Her voice is sharp, full of authority.

She's my rival in every sense. Even if I was okay with her suggestion, I wouldn't let her win this easily.

I lean in, our faces inches apart until she can feel the power of every word I say to her.

"We aren't done, baby. I did you a favor. I killed for you. There was a time I would have done it for free, but not anymore. Now you owe me a debt."

Her nostrils flare, her pupils dilate, and her heartbeat jumps in her throat.

I drag my eyes down her body one last time—over her perfect blonde curls, down her sharp clavicles to her full breasts, over her lace-covered stomach, drooling as I continue down her hips to the slit revealing her toned legs. She's every man's dream—but she's my nightmare.

"I'll pay you whatever you want."

I shake my head. "I don't want your money."

She takes a shuttered breath. I have no doubt that her panties are soaked.

I let my eyes darken. I let my voice deepen. I let every bit of the menacing beast inside me roar to life. The part of me that scares most people, but will only turn Liesel on even more.

That will confuse her even more than she's already perplexed.

She thinks I came for her, and I did. She's terrified of what I could do to her. And she should be because I'll take more than she can ever imagine.

"You owe me a debt, Liesel Dunn. You've owed me a debt for a long time. And soon, I plan on collecting."

7

LIESEL

I owe Langston a debt.

He thought those words would scare me. He thought he could just demand I give him whatever he wants because he killed for me.

I don't think so.

He calls me huntress, but I'm so much more—lawyer, badass woman, queen. I don't take orders from anyone. I don't owe anyone. Especially not an egotistical man on a power trip who negated our agreement when he killed Fitz instead of letting me do it like we agreed.

As far as I'm concerned, I owe him nothing for what he did. He didn't keep to our verbal contract.

I'd be willing to pay him for his time, nothing more.

And as for any past debts I owe him, he can suck it. Our past stays in the past.

There is no way he's going to start collecting on old debts. If he does, then it means I get to collect too, and he owes me as much or more than I owe him.

But I know what Langston really wants. The same thing he's always wanted.

51

Me.

My body.

My soul.

He wants to control me. He wants to boss me around in the bedroom.

No way in hell am I letting that happen.

Not just because I'd be cheating on Waylon if I did. Langston doesn't deserve that part of me—ever.

And the only person left on this earth who terrifies me is Langston.

"You're all worked up, my love," Waylon says, kissing my shoulder.

He's right. He can read me well when I get worked up like this. My body is hot and agitated and horny. *God, I'm so horny.*

Sure, Langston turned me on. He's a blonde god in a tux. He looked like a hotter James Bond. I've seen Langston a lot of ways—T-shirt and shorts, shirtless in swim trunks, even naked. But it's a rare occasion to see him in a tux or suit. He hates them.

Yet, he can wear a tux with the best of them. He fits into the world of powerful men, whether he wants to or not. All he has to do to belong is get a respectable job and wear a suit or tux with pride.

But that's something Langston will never do. He'd rather take orders from his best friend. Protect and serve—that's Langston.

I used to like it, especially when he was protecting me. But I lost that right a long time ago. And apparently, now I have to pay him back when he protects me.

Ugh, how annoying.

The elevator doors open to Waylon's penthouse. He has an early flight tomorrow, which is why we are staying here tonight instead of my place. People used to think it was weird that we both still have our own places, but both places are incredible; it would be a shame to give either of them up. We can easily afford both. And they are located across town from each other, which makes it convenient to stay at one or the other depending on our schedules.

"You think you can help me work off some steam?" I ask, running my tongue over my bottom lip.

His eyes light up with anticipation. He loses his stone, distinguished expression, and turns into a horny boy willing to please me—just the way I like it. Some women prefer a man who dominates them in the bedroom, one who ties them up, spanks them, bosses them around.

Not me—that all seems too degrading. I like the power. I like to be the boss.

Maybe it's because of my history.

Maybe it's because of who I am.

Either way, it's the only way I fuck—I'm the one who dominates.

Waylon unlocks the front door and holds it open for me.

I grab his tie as I walk past and yank him inside before slamming him against the wall, already feeling a tiny bit better now that I'm going to get a dozen orgasms tonight to make up for what Langston said and did.

"Yea, baby, use me. Hurt me. Take out your anger and pent up emotion on me. I want to know how badly you want me, because it can't be as much as I want you," Waylon says, kissing my neck sweetly.

I smirk. He has no idea about my past, but he does know that I'm fucked up.

And then I remember the cameras.

There are more in Waylon's place than in mine. Here there are even cameras in the bedroom.

Waylon is paranoid, and his one fetish is watching us fuck

over and over. There is even a mirror on the ceiling so he can have a better view.

Where there are cameras, there is Langston. I know he's tapped into the security feed. I know he's watching, which makes this all the more fun.

Langston thinks he can demand I repay my debt to him by giving him my body. I'll show him exactly what he's missing, exactly what he'll never have.

"Kneel," I say.

Waylon looks up at me excitedly. He may like ordering people around in the boardroom, but here, he likes me bossing him.

I look up at the camera in the entryway corner.

I reach around my back and unzip my dress. Then I let the straps fall off my shoulders, before wiggling my hips as I push the dress to a pile on the floor.

I'm wearing nothing but heels and black lacy lingerie—bra, thong, and garter.

"Lick me. Make me come."

Waylon's eyes brighten. He loves making me come, but this isn't for him. This is for Langston, to show him what he will never taste. What he will never have.

Waylon's hands slide up the length of my long legs, and I focus on his touch instead of staring into the camera. Langston already knows that I know he's watching. Now to revel in the feeling of ecstasy as Waylon worships my body in a way that Langston never will.

His fingers hook into the bands of my thong, and he carefully slides it down my body, his brooding eyes locked on his prize as he drops my panties to the floor in a pile on top of my dress.

He licks his lips like he's about to devour his favorite food. Waylon is a lot of things; he has a lot of traits I like about him. But this might be what I like the most.

"Waylon, lick me," I command, my voice raspy in anticipation of him eating me out.

He grins at the desperation in my voice and then does as I order. His arms wrap around my hips as his tongue licks the length of my slit, tasting the sweetness of my arousal. He moans, sending vibrations through my body.

My body shudders, and I grab onto his head for support as he licks over me. Tasting, teasing until he's making me pant at a pace that rivals any exercise routine I've ever had.

"You taste so fucking good. I can't believe I'm the one who gets to taste you. The only one."

I grin as my hands sink deeper into his hair, gripping him so fucking hard that I should be afraid I'm going to rip his hair out. I'm not, though; Waylon can take it.

I do let my eyes roll up to the camera at Waylon's words. *You hear that, Langston? Waylon's the only one who gets to taste me like this.*

And then, he's pushing his fingers inside me. He's not gentle, but not rough enough to spark nightmares of my past. It's just enough to make my body explode in a rolling orgasm that is just the start of my night.

"Yes!" I scream, not using his name yet. After all, I'm the woman in control here. One orgasm isn't enough for him to earn hearing me call out his name. Not yet.

Waylon removes his fingers after I've come down from my orgasm. Then he licks his fingers, savoring every drop of my cum on his fingers.

"Stand and go to the bedroom. Undress and get ready to fuck my brains out."

Waylon stands and gives me the softest of kisses on the lips, reminding me, as if I could forget, how incredible his kisses are. Promising me that he's going to fuck me better than any fantasy I could ever imagine.

Waylon is breathtakingly sexy as he walks to our bedroom while still wearing a tux and my cum on his lips.

This is the life I always imagined but never thought I could get.

When Waylon is gone, I walk to the fridge, still wearing my heels, bra, and garter.

I grab a water bottle from the fridge and take a sip while I wait for Waylon to get undressed and ready for me.

It gives me a moment alone with Langston.

I take my time removing the bobby pins, holding my curls to one side until my hair is down. I run my hands through them to loosen the curls before taking one last sip of water.

"He's mine. And I'm no one's. You hear me, Langston? I belong to myself." I glare at the camera with the full force of warrior about to go into battle. I know that Langston won't back down easily.

But I just won the first battle. And I'm about to put an arrow through his heart with what I have planned the rest of the night. When I fuck—I fuck all night. I fuck until I can't move, can't think—until all I feel is the thousands of tiny nerve endings exploding from waves of pleasure beating through my body.

I fuck to forget.

I fuck to feel alive.

I fuck like it's what I was made to do.

"You will never have me," I whisper into the dark before I strut down the hallway to the bedroom where Waylon waits for me.

He's done what I asked. He's undressed. Condom is already on his hard dick. And he's lying face-up on the bed, the handcuffs ready for me to use on him.

He's ready to be dominated.

He's ready to give me what I need, and take what he needs.

I'm not sure if this is love or something like it—but I never feel happier than I do in moments like this where I can take complete control. I love that I don't have to fight him, that he just follows my orders.

I walk over to the bed silently. His eyes follow me. I'm sure Langston's eyes follow too.

I never thought I was one to enjoy having another watch me fuck, but the heat spreading through my body is like nothing I've ever felt before. So maybe I like being watched. It's something I'll have to explore after I deal with my Langston problem.

I grab Waylon's wrist and pull it up until I can lock the first handcuff around it, tying him to the poster bed. And then I kiss the palm of his hand as he lets me tie him up.

"Good boy," I say.

His eyes roll back at my soothing words. I may dominate, but it's not about pain. It's not about hurting Waylon. I just want the control—no, I need it. I can't fuck without it. I can't be in a relationship without complete control.

I have trust issues.

But it's also my greatest strength. I don't need a man to make me feel wanted or powerful. All I need is me.

I repeat the same binding to his other wrist and both of his ankles. He's tied up and ready for me to fuck him. He can't hurt me. He can't touch me. And unlike me, Waylon trusts me completely.

I climb up onto the bed as I kiss up his body. His thick, muscled thighs from all the weight lifting he does. His hard condom covered cock. He's hard and ready for me, but I lick up and down his shaft to feel as turned on as possible, as wet as I can get before I fuck him.

I vowed to myself a long time ago that I wouldn't let sex ever be painful—not ever again. He knows I won't fuck him until I'm completely drenched and have already come at least twice.

I continue my teasing up his rippled abs, his strong chest, and chiseled jaw.

"Make me come," I say as I straddle his face, my pussy hovering over him.

"My pleasure, my love."

He lifts his head to feast between my legs while I grab the headboard for support with one hand while my other plays with my breasts, freeing them from the lace bra and then rolling my thumb over one of my nipples. I shift my hips back and forth over his face to increase the friction as I get riled up again.

My mind flickers to Langston, watching me come apart. I shouldn't even let him see this part of me. He shouldn't get to see me orgasm.

But it's not about him. This is about me. About taking control of my own body. I want to show him this incredible experience he'll never get.

Finally, my body is coaxed into another orgasm.

As soon as I come down enough to move, I slide down Walon's body, grab his cock, and push him inside my slick walls.

He curses as he fills me tightly with his long, thick rod.

My nails dig into his chest as the pleasure fills me, and I lock my eyes with Waylon.

I won't think about Langston again, not until I'm finished with Waylon, which won't be until he has to leave for his flight in the morning.

Waylon reads my mind, knowing exactly how intense sex can get with me, how long it can last. He's on board and has the stamina to keep up with me. I'm going to need release after release to get me through an entire week without sex.

Langston may get to watch, but he doesn't get me. He

doesn't get my attention, my thoughts, and definitely not my body—my orgasms. Those are all for Waylon and me.

I start off slow, getting my rhythm, and then Waylon's hips start thrusting with me. My body glides over his, my clit hitting the point of his hard, sculpted V, and soon I'm convulsing around him as he pours his cum into the condom within me.

"Waylon!" I finally scream, making it clear that he's the only man for me.

I climb off of him and remove the condom as I walk to the bathroom, still wearing my power, 'fuck me' heels.

I am a goddess; three orgasms is nowhere near enough to satisfy me.

I grab the box of condoms in the bathroom and bring them to the bed before I untie Waylon. I want to be fucked in every position. Now that I've established my authority, my need, my control, Waylon will respect my power.

"Fuck me from behind. I want to be fucked in every position, in every way, until the sun comes up. Think you can handle that, baby?"

He smirks. "For you, I'd do anything."

He rolls a condom on, then grabs my hips, and carefully slides between my legs as he fills me and reaches around to stroke my clit.

My eyes roll back at the feeling. This is the life. This is my life. This is what I chose. And I won't ever let a man take anything from me ever again.

8

LANGSTON

FUCK, Liesel.

She knew I was watching.

That was complete torture for me.

Fuck.

Fuck.

FUCK!

My blood pressure soared to a thousand over a million watching her get fucked by that cocksucker.

The message was clear, though—she's his, not mine.

I laugh at that.

She thinks she won.

Sure, she pissed me off to no end. No amount of jacking off has brought me down from my pent up frustration.

She has no idea what I want from her, but I'm going to enjoy showing her.

Soon, my huntress, I'll be coming to collect my debt. And your little show just made collecting my debt that much sweeter.

9

LIESEL

Not many men have the stamina to go all night.

Waylon does.

Sure, his cock needed a few minutes to rest between each round, which was when he put his lips and tongue to good use. He knows how to pleasure me all night.

Just staying awake all night is a feat. Waylon never let my brain go anywhere except the intense pleasure I was feeling.

Then he was sweet enough to pour me a heaping cup of coffee and set it on the nightstand in one of those self-heating cups so it would be warm and ready for me when I woke up—which was about an hour after I fell asleep.

I don't need much sleep after a night like that. Nights like last night are what I live for.

I stretch, feeling how sore my muscles are.

I smile at the comforting ache. I don't have a need to workout. Sex with Waylon like this a couple of times a week gives me more stamina than running or biking or pilates ever could.

I take my time finishing my coffee before heading to the shower.

I walk naked into the en-suite bathroom that is larger than most people's bedrooms, especially in New York City.

I flip the shower on and immediately step in, the cold water soothing my aching muscles.

Most people prefer warm showers. Not me; cold showers wake me up and keep my skin youthful far more than warm showers. I grew up taking cold showers; we rarely had enough heat for warm ones, and it's a habit that's stuck.

It's one of the reasons Waylon and I hardly ever shower together.

My mind starts to wander as I close my eyes and wash my hair.

I think about the dozens of orgasms I received last night. I think about how high I feel, the happy hormones pulsing through my veins. I think about Waylon, about how he looked, sounded, and felt as he drove inside me.

But I don't let my mind go free. I don't let it wander to who I really want to be thinking about.

I get a sudden chill down my spine, but I don't turn the water warmer. Eventually, the feeling fades.

I know a lot of time has passed when I finally step out of the shower with a towel wrapped around my body onto the heated bathroom floors. It always shocks me every time when I step out. Somehow I always forget about that feature when I look at the marble floor.

And then I look up, and my heart skips.

The mirror has fogged over, and there are three words written in the fog.

Five More Days.

I quickly glance around the bathroom, but there is nowhere for someone to hide.

Did Waylon come back?

Did he leave a message on the mirror before he left?

No, that can't be. Waylon is only going to be gone for three days.

I dart out of the bathroom and into the bedroom. I still don't find anyone.

In fact, I run through the entire condo and find no one.

I could call our security team, but I don't.

I don't need to.

I know who left the message.

The only man who could have snuck in and out without security spotting him.

A man I thought I had made perfectly clear to last night that I was not his. That I don't owe him anything.

Langston Pearce.

I know how our security team didn't catch Langston, but I don't know how I didn't notice myself.

Even with my eyes closed, I always know when Langston is nearby.

The chills—that was Langston.

I did know. I just didn't let myself acknowledge it.

I walk back to the bedroom just as I hear my cell phone buzzing on the nightstand.

I jump at the sudden sound, and slowly walk over, assuming it's Langston who's calling and he can wait.

But when I pick the phone up, it's Kai on the caller ID.

I sigh and almost decide not to answer the call, but she'll keep calling the rest of the day, especially if Langston put her up to it.

"Kai, now really isn't a good time. I have to meet with a client in an hour, and I'm already running late," I answer, not giving her a chance to speak first. Kai is the only one who continues to keep in touch even when I insist I no longer want to be part of that life, that family.

There was once a time when I loved being the only woman among three dangerous men—Enzo, Zeke, and

Langston. I was their entire focus. I thought I would end up with Enzo, the leader, but I realized too late that that was never meant to be. Enzo ended up with Kai.

I'm not bitter. They belong together, but my life changed after that. Everyone pushed me to Langston like they thought we needed our own happily ever after. None of them know our true history. None of them know our past.

And then Zeke found Siren, and the pressure increased for Langston and me.

But I don't want a happily ever after.

I don't want to live in their dangerous world.

And I don't need friends, especially girlfriends—I'm a lone wolf.

"Then I'll keep it short. Siren and I are going on a pampered girls vacation to Santorini for a week, and we'd love for you to come with us. We are leaving in two weeks, I know it's short notice, but hopefully, you can get someone to cover your clients for you."

"I—" I start.

"You are not giving me some excuse why you can't come right now. I have two weeks to convince you to go, and I want to spend every day of that persuading you. We haven't seen you in six months, and we miss you."

I sigh. "I'll think about it."

I have no idea how to get out of this. A girl's trip sounds like my nightmare. Kai and Siren are nice enough, but to be trapped on an island with them for an entire week of gossiping, drinking, and sunshine?

No, thanks.

I wouldn't survive a week with them.

Kai squeals excitedly like I just said yes, instead of blowing her off like I did.

"I have to go," I say.

"Of course, will talk to you tomorrow!"

I end the call. Kai is going to keep to her word and call me every day this week. And then again the next week. There is no stopping her once she gets going. She's the boss for a reason. Her orders are followed, no exception.

I don't have a clue how to get out of this.

I walk back into the bathroom and look at the words again—*five more days.*

The words have started to fade, and soon they won't exist at all. Then I'll be second-guessing myself, thinking I made it up.

Five.

More.

Days.

What will Langston demand of me then?

I have an idea—and I suspect I just found out my excuse for why I can't go on the girl's trip. I'm with Langston—that would shut Kai up. She wouldn't dare interfere if she thought there was a chance that Langston and I could get together. She knows nothing about my life here. She doesn't know about Waylon.

Langston has a plan to extract a debt from me in five days.

I smirk as I drop the towel, knowing that Langston is watching.

I'm not going to wait five days. I'm done waiting, and I'm done playing by his rules. This is going to end much sooner than five days.

LANGSTON

LIESEL THINKS she's going to win.

Not this time.

We've been fighting since we were kids. Fighting an invisible war with each other—one that was never spoken about. One that neither of us knew the terms, rules, or even what we would win. We just knew that we had to win.

Since we were five, we've been fighting, hurting, deceiving one another.

Why?

Because hurt people, hurt people. And we've been damaged more in our youth than any of our friends could imagine.

Our battles didn't always involve hurting one another. Although, that was the majority of what happened.

We were enemies—usually fighting and angry at each other. Liesel was chasing my best friend, Enzo, and I thought she was annoying. So I would tease her, piss her off. That's how our relationship started.

Later as we grew into horny teenagers, the lust started.

The attraction grew, but I was beneath her. She was after Enzo, the man with power, not me—his side-kick.

The lust turned to sexual frustration and then serious feelings we both had no right to feel, which just pissed us both off more. We both knew from a very young age that we could never ever be together.

If we could have escaped each other, if we could have never met, we would have. As much as we needed to stay apart, the world kept pushing us back together over and over again.

Things have changed.

We can't keep living our lives like this. We can't keep battling forever. This war has to end. This is the start of our end.

It's not going to be easy for either of us, but it's necessary.

We've both been holding onto secrets for too long, since I ripped half of that envelope out of her hand—it's time.

Neither of us will give up our truths easily. We will fight with our lies until the bitter end. Until one of us finally breaks down, until one of us loses.

But as soon as either of us speaks the truth—that will be the end of us.

We will no longer be friends.

We will never have a shot at being lovers.

We won't even be enemies anymore.

We will be out of each other's lives for good.

Which is why I'll drag out this final game as long as I can. I'm not ready to let go of Liesel yet.

I smirk when I see Liesel on the security camera in the lobby of the hotel I'm staying at. It seems that Liesel is ready for this to be over faster than I am.

She doesn't get to be in control of this.

She doesn't get to win.

She's an excellent hunter. She can seek whatever and

whoever she wants. There is nothing that can be hidden from her.

She found me—four days earlier than I'm ready to be found.

So I won't let her find me.

She is a great hunter, but she's rusty. She's been away from danger for far too long.

I, on the other hand, never left the darkness. Over the last year, I've only let it deeper into my soul until I've become as evil as the world I was born into.

She can hunt all she wants, but she'll only find me when I'm ready to be found. She should have learned that by now.

I watch on my computer as Liesel walks to the elevator in a tight red dress and heels. She came straight from the office. In the last month that I've been following her, I've never seen her out of her dress or heels outside of her condo, and she makes no exception today.

She likes the dresses and heels so much because it's her suit of armor. It protects her and makes her more powerful. It's not because she's a girlie girl. She doesn't love always being so dressed up. She just likes the power she's able to wield while dolled up.

I take a quick glance around the hotel room as she rides up in the elevator to see if there is anything lying out that I don't want her to see, but there isn't. I already know that without looking. I travel light. All of my stuff is already in my backpack.

I close my laptop and stick it into my backpack before zipping it up.

I pull out my cell and switch the feed to my phone. I watch her exit the elevator with complete confidence like she belongs here.

I have thirty seconds until she makes it to my room. I spot a pen and paper on the desk and scribble on it before I move to the bed. I lift the ceiling tile, and pull myself up just as I hear her scan the hotel keycard she flirted her way into getting.

The tile pops back in place before she opens the door, and I switch the feed on my phone until I'm tapped into the security in my own room.

This is what I do for a living—security. I design security systems for the wealthy. Usually, on yachts or mansions, but it gives me the skills to tap into the best-designed systems.

Liesel's eyes flitter around the room.

"You couldn't stay in a nicer place, huh, Langston?" she asks to the room as she wanders around, looking under the bed and then in the bathroom to see if I'm hiding anywhere.

I smile at her words, though. She knows even if I'm not here that I'm watching. I'm always watching. It's the only way to protect everyone I love.

Not that she falls into that category anymore.

After a half-hearted attempt to find me in the room, Liesel walks over to the piece of paper I left for her.

"Four more days," Liesel reads out loud.

She balls the piece of paper up and tosses it into the wastebasket under the desk before her eyes scan the room one last time for any clues as to where I am or where I could have gone.

Her eyes flit up to the ceiling, and I almost think she might have found me. She starts talking, and I realize she's found the security camera in the corner so she can look into my eyes as she speaks.

"I don't owe you anything, Langston Pearce. And you won't be demanding anything of me in four days. You won't be taking me. You don't own me. You will take nothing from me."

She licks her red lips, knowing that her lips are my favorite thing about her.

How I've wanted to kiss her lips. There have been so many opportunities throughout my life where I could have kissed her, but something always held me back. I've never tasted them—never tasted the poisonous, tempting red apple lips.

She knows her seduction won't work on me. And yet, she still does it, driving me mad.

"I gave you a chance to end this war, to talk face to face. You ran, hid. I'm usually the hunter, the seeker. And you follow me in order to kill. But not this time. This time, I'm going to hide, and you'll have to do the hunting.

"And if all these years of hunting have taught me one thing, it's that I know how to hide better than anyone. You'll never find me unless I want to be found. You aren't going to win, Langston. So surrender, and maybe I'll let you live."

With that, she walks out. Her fighting words hit me in the chest as hard as a bullet.

Liesel thinks she can hide.

She thinks she has power.

She has no idea of the truth.

It's impossible to hide from someone whose heart you stole when we were five. That piece of me she stole calls out to me no matter where she goes. I won't have to hunt her to find her; I just have to follow the beacon, the signal that she involuntarily sends to me.

She can't hide any more than I can. And in four days she'll be mine. I just don't know what I'm going to do with her when I claim her.

LIESEL

MY PLAN DIDN'T WORK. Of course, Langston, king of security, saw me coming on the cameras. I knew he would see me the second I walked into the hotel. Hotels are full of cameras, which makes it impossible to sneak up on Langston. He can hack into any system. He sees everything.

I shiver at that thought, of all the things he's seen. Things he's seen and done nothing about.

Four days.

That's how long I have until he comes after me to extract a debt he thinks I owe him. I still don't know why he thinks I owe him for killing one man for me. He's killed dozens of men for me when we were younger. *Before...*

Before he tore my secrets from my grip.

He won't let me find him before the four days are up.

But I'm not going to let him take me in four days. I'd rather hide the rest of my life than let Langston win.

I'm not going to have to hide the rest of my life, though—just for four more days.

If I can stay hidden, away from Langston's reach for four days, then I win. He may still come for me. He still may come to collect his debt after four days, but he will have lost. He will lose his power, his upper hand.

He knows that, that's why the timing is so important to him. He wants complete control over me, he always has. He's been trying to boss me around since we were ten.

I start my Porsche and head back to my apartment to think in the comfort of my own home. I blast the radio as I drive, trying not to think about Langston, the best way for my ideas to flow.

The problem with Langston being able to see everything is that I can't write anything down. I can't look anything up on my computer. I can't make plans except in my head.

When I get to my condo, I pour myself a glass of scotch while avoiding looking up at the security camera. I refuse to talk to Langston anymore if he's too much of a coward to show his face. I won't let him into my mind either. From now on, he only gets to see what I want him to see. And he sure as hell won't be getting another glimpse of my body.

I swirl the liquid in my glass as I contemplate my choices. I can hide in plain sight or hide at the ends of the earth. Anything less means he will win—he'll find me.

An idea forms.

It may not work, but at least I'll go out fighting. I won't make Langston's job easy.

It wouldn't shock me at all if Enzo and Kai put Langston up to this thinking they could drag me kicking and screaming back to their world, back into that life. I won't do it. I'd rather die than go back.

I pick up my phone and dial Waylon's number.

"Hey, sweetheart, miss me already?"

I smile at his response. "I always miss you."

I hear the clinking of ice. "You enjoying a glass of scotch?"

"Yes, same as you."

I can feel his grin through the phone. We always drink

scotch together. It's one of the many things Waylon and I have in common.

"Unfortunately, you're going to have to miss me for a while longer."

"And why's that?"

"Some old girlfriends invited me on a girl's trip to Santorini, and I had to push up a business trip before I meet them, so it will be three weeks until I'm home."

"A girl's trip, huh? I thought I was your only friend?" he teases.

"You are, you know that."

"I think a girl's trip would be good for you. You work too hard; it's time you got a little vacation. Where is your business trip? I might be able to meet up with you before you go, but my schedule is crazy these next couple of weeks as well."

"Sacramento and then Chicago."

He sighs. "I'm in Houston and then Hong Kong."

"It will just make our reunion in three weeks all that more enjoyable," I let my voice drop into a raspiness that turns him on.

"You're going to need to take off another week when you get back. I'm going to need that long to show you how much I'll miss you."

My panties soak, and my nipples peak up at that thought. "Deal."

I end the call, and then I call my assistant Gerald.

"What can I do for you, Miss Dunn?"

"Can you book me a flight to Tokyo and then a private jet in Tokyo to take me wherever I might need to go next?"

"Of course. When would you like to go?"

"Tomorrow afternoon, please."

"I'll book you a first-class flight to Tokyo and arrange the usual private jet for you to be ready at your beck and call after you arrive. I'll email you the details as usual."

"Thank you, Gerald."

"You're welcome, Miss Dunn."

I end the call. I just gave Langston two separate leads to follow, and I'm about to give him a dozen more. He'll have no idea where I'm going when I'm through with him.

I book more commercial and private flights on my own.

I book bus tickets.

I rent cars.

I rent yachts.

I spend more money in a single hour than most people do in a lifetime, arranging dozens of leads that Langston will be forced to check up on.

And then I call Tiffany.

"Liesel! I'm so glad you called, it's been too long."

I love her enthusiasm. She's a struggling actress I met at the beauty salon years ago, and she's always looking to pick up extra money. Plus, she has a very particular skillset that has come in handy a handful of times before.

She's not a great actress, but she's good enough to play me when she needs to. It helps, that with the right makeup, she looks exactly like me. That's her real skillset—doing makeup. I've tried to convince her to become a makeup artist, but she's always resisted.

"Can you meet me at the salon tomorrow? I need someone to help me with my makeup," I ask, providing our shared clue that I will be needing her services as discreetly as possible.

"Absolutely."

***

I pull Tiffany into the bathroom of the salon before we have our hair done.

"You have a job for me?" Tiffany asks with hope.

I look her up and down. She's skinnier than the last time I saw her. Her hair is a disheveled mess.

"Yes, I do."

She lights up with a bright smile.

"I need you to take a one week trip as me; I'll pay for everything."

"Where to?"

"Where would you like to go?"

"Paris!"

I laugh. "Paris it is then. If you want to check out London, Rome, Barcelona, or any other city while you're in Europe, go for it. I'll pay you a hundred grand in addition to the trip expenses."

"Oh my god, that's too much to just take a vacation."

"No, it's not."

"Will I be in danger?"

I shake my head. "The man who is after me won't hurt me. And he will have no reason to harm you either." *At least, I don't think Langston will hurt me.*

"But we have to make the switch right now. We have to change clothes, you have to drive my car with my cell phone and credit cards to the airport right now, and I'll have to go back to your place."

She frowns. "Um…you don't want to go back to my place."

"Why?"

"Because my place is a closet with a door that doesn't lock, cockroaches, and no hot water."

I smile. "That's perfect."

A place like that won't have any working security cameras. There will be no way for Langston to follow me. And hopefully, he'll be chasing Tiffany halfway around the world anyway.

We quickly swap clothes, and I tie my hair up in a messy

bun. I start tying her broken tennis shoes that are two sizes too big on me, while she fastens on the straps of my heels.

But even dressed in jeans and a T-shirt and her in a dress and heels, I still look like I come from Beverly Hills, and she looks like she hasn't gotten a decent night's sleep in months.

I pull a wet wipe from my purse and wipe the makeup from my face before I hand my purse to her. She digs through and starts applying makeup that makes her freakishly look exactly like me. When she's done, she turns and looks at me.

"How do I look?" she asks with big eyes.

I let my eyes drag up and down her body, looking for any tiny details that will tip-off Langston right away.

"You look perfect," I say with a tight smile. "Now remember how I said you should act when you're playing me?"

"Like a bad bitch who isn't afraid of anyone and looks up to no one.'

"Exactly."

I feel around in my pockets. All I have is a twenty-dollar bill, her ID, and a pay-as-you-go phone to get me through the next part.

"I'm going to go. But you stay and get your hair done however you like before you leave. What's your address?"

She gives me directions to her place, which will either cost the entire twenty dollars I have in bus fares to get there, or I'm going to be taking the subway—something I haven't done in years. But now isn't the time to get grossed out by how half of New Yorkers live.

I thank Tiffany one last time, and then I sneak out the back door of the hair salon while Tiffany struts out into the front.

I look around for any way that Langston could be following me, but I don't see any cameras or any people.

This will work.

Three subway trains later, I finally make it to my stop, which is still a good ten-block walk away from the apartment. Thankfully, I have tennis shoes instead of heels. For the first time that I can remember, I let my head fall a little. I let my shoulders slump. I feel less than I actually am. And for once, it feels good to not have to worry about anything. To not have to worry about power or control. To just be.

When I make it to Tiffany's apartment building, the sight of a crumbling building and cockroaches does nothing to deter me. I head inside to the third floor and then collapse onto her stained mattress on the floor. She doesn't have a pillow, just a ratty old blanket.

Regardless, I will rest well, because tomorrow I have to do something much worse than sleep in an unsafe apartment with no air conditioning or pillow. Tomorrow I have to go back to where my life began, to where the nightmares started. That is the one place Langston thinks I'd never go.

The next day, I wake up early. The sounds of people yelling and alarms blasting fills my room even though I'm in the apartment alone.

I don't know how Tiffany lives like this. I hope the money I gave her is enough to start a new life.

I rinse off in her cold, broken shower. I change into sweatpants and a sweatshirt I find in her closet but keep the same tennis shoes. Lastly, I start the long subway journey to the pier.

After several train switches, I make it to my boat rental.

My heart freezes at the sight of the boat. It's modest, nothing like the yachts of the family I grew up next to but never truly in. My mother worked for a dangerous man as a maid. I grew up with that dangerous man's son, Enzo, and his friends Zeke and Langston. I know how to operate a boat. I know the benefits and dangers.

I just never thought I'd willingly step onto one.

"Do you know how to operate this thing, miss?" the man in overalls and a bandana asks.

I smile as I take the keys from him. "Better than you do."

His eyes widen, and then he chuckles like there is no way a woman like me knows how to operate a boat better than him—*misogynist*.

I start untying the boat before he's even stepped off, and then I start the engines, forcing the man to jump back onto the pier.

I wave at him with my adorable, shameless smile, letting him know how much of a catch I truly am beneath the ratty clothes, but he'll never get me. Then I peel out in the boat, taking off hard and fast and letting the breeze run through my hair.

Langston used to be a knight in the sea. He used to monitor every boat, every passenger in the ocean. But he won't be looking for me here. The boat I rented isn't under my name, and I didn't use any money tied to me to pay for it. It will take a lot of digging on Langston's part to find me.

Three days.

I have three days until Langston comes for me.

It will take two to make it to Miami, where I grew up. Where I met the boy who shone brighter than the sun. I'm tired of living in his shadow. In three days, we end this.

———

I drive the boat straight through day and night. I don't sleep. *Thank God I've learned to operate without that basic need.*

I'd forgotten how thrilling it is to be driving a boat by

myself with nothing but the lights of shore and the stars overhead. I'd forgotten how bumpy the waves feel when you're alone in a boat. They feel ten times as intense as they really are. I'd forgotten how eery the calm quietness of the ocean seems with only the waves knocking against my boat, reminding me of how quickly the sea can turn dangerous.

But even being here, I'm still not called back to this life. I'd rather be anywhere but here. The ocean hasn't been kind to me.

I get to Miami as the sun rises on the third day, the day that Langston says he's coming for me. But if I succeeded, today will come and go without a word from Langston.

I dock the boat, and then I walk down the pier, the sun already heating me as I walk, making me want to strip out my clothes and into a bikini, but I won't. Not today. Today is about hiding, not being seen.

I rent a car from the car rental down the street; then, I drive to the house I grew up in.

No, that's not true. The house I grew up in was Enzo's guest house, and that house burned to the ground.

No, I drive to the house my mother lived in when she wasn't working. The house I lived in until I was ten but barely remember.

The house we fought in.

The house I begged her to take me away from, to move anywhere but here. She did as we asked. We moved, and my life turned upside down in one night. Forever changed, all because of where we moved to and who my mother worked for.

She couldn't be a teacher or a hairstylist or a maid in a hotel. No, she had to be a maid for a man who took whatever he wanted with no regard for life. No regard for conse-quences.

I never thought I'd be back in Miami, let alone the tiny

one-bedroom home that I once shared with my mother. That was when I wasn't sleeping at Enzo's or even Langston's. I did anything I could to avoid coming here when I lived here. I never thought I'd visit now that I'm an adult with options.

Still, it's the place I feel my mom the most. I should have visited before, but I just couldn't.

"Hey, Mom. You've been taking care of the old place?" I ask to the sky as I walk inside. My mom died from an overdose the same night I learned that my jackass father was still alive on my eighteenth birthday.

The house is empty. There is no furniture. No sign any human has stepped foot in here since the time my mom lived here.

I sigh and look at Tiffany's phone. It's nine o'clock in the morning. I have a long time to wait.

Thankfully, I have my nightmares to keep me company.

I sit on the floor in the corner of the living room, and I wait, hoping my hiding spot is good enough to hide from the devil.

Two minutes left until midnight.

Two minutes left until I win.

That's when I hear the car. The slamming of a door shut. The honk of the horn as he locks the car. The heavy footsteps as he approaches the house.

Langston's here.

I know it without looking up as the front door opens.

He found me.

"You've gotten better at hide and seek, I see," Langston frowns at me.

"And you've become more of a monster," I shoot back.

LANGSTON

I ALMOST LOST.

I almost didn't find her in time.

Liesel almost won.

Almost...

It wouldn't have really mattered if I didn't find her the day I said I would. The game we play is invisible, with invisible rules, and invisible rewards. We are playing a game without all the pieces, without knowing how close the other is to winning, without even knowing if we are playing the same game or different games.

But we do know one thing—we both share lies. Lies that keep us from freedom, from living the life we want.

It's time to end this.

Time to finally finish our game.

To have a winner.

Our game is nothing like Enzo and Kai's game was with official rules and an empire to gain at the end.

Our game is nothing like Zeke and Siren's game, spilling sinful truths that harm more than they help.

Our game is simple: lie until you can't lie anymore. Try to get the upper hand. Try to get the other to fold first.

That's what having control of this meeting was about. We were always going to eventually meet. But on whose terms —*mine or hers?*

I got here just in the nick of time. I won this round.

But Liesel has gotten more skilled than I give her credit for. She may live a cushy life now, yet that doesn't mean she hasn't been honing her skills on the side.

She put out fake leads, trying to throw me off her trail, so I had no choice but to consider every lead. There was no way for her to hide once she decided to board a plane, car, or boat. She couldn't hide from me; she never could.

I thought I had found her when she boarded a plane to Paris. Of course, she would choose the most extravagant, beautiful place to try and hide. She wouldn't take one of the dozens of flights she booked to the middle of nowhere.

I boarded my own flight and followed her to Paris. To my surprise, I found a woman who looks strikingly like Liesel and yet isn't. They could be twins if I didn't know that Liesel has no siblings, no family. She gave up her family.

Once I arrived and realized my mistake, I only had hours left to find Liesel before my time was up. I had followed all the leads she left for me. I searched all the surveillance at every airport, bridge out of the city, bus stop, harbor and found no sight of her.

I wasn't going to find her via my usual routes. She slipped by undetected. My only choice was to choose one last place to search for her. She could have been anywhere, but that's when I realized where she had chosen. The one place I knew she'd never go. My own backyard.

Miami.

Her mother's house specifically.

Now, I'm standing in the small, broken-down room face to face with Liesel.

I say room, because this has never been a house, definitely never a home. It's barely big enough for two people to breathe in comfortably. A strong wind would knock the whole building down.

Liesel hardly stepped a foot inside her mother's home growing up, and it surprises me the strength it took her to come back here to Miami—the place that ruined both of our lives.

"You win, okay? You win," Liesel finally says, the pain etched around the edges of her voice. She hates losing as much as I do.

I take a closer look at her. She looks like she's been on the run for months instead of days. This is the first time in decades that I've seen her in anything less than designer clothes. She's usually radiating confidence and beauty. Right now, the oversized rags that cling to her body scream homeless.

She did everything she could to avoid me. To escape, hide, and prevent me from winning. I should compliment her on her hard work, but I won't. I like watching her squirm.

I glare down at her as I step further into the small room, forcing her to stand and step back to avoid me touching her. She hates showing defeat, but she hates me touching her more.

"What do you want, Langston? I'm tired of our game." Her eyes drag up my body in my dark jeans and a fitted gray shirt.

"Really? Then why did you run? You know the only way to end our game is to finish it. Declare a winner once and for all. But we can't finish the game if we keep avoiding each other."

She shakes her head as the corner of her lip rises into a smirk. "You have no idea what finishing the game means."

"Maybe. Or maybe I know more than you could imagine." We talk in circles, neither of us speaking the truth. Neither of us showing the other our cards. Neither of us showing the other the final move we need to make to win.

"You owe me a debt, my huntress."

"I already offered to pay you for that debt, even though you don't deserve it. The arrangement was that I would kill the man, you would just be present to give me plausible deniability." She pauses for effect. "Instead, you murdered him."

I pet my chin, staring at her, as she continues to pout and throw a mini tantrum, reneging on our agreement. She's forgotten our deal. One we made a long time ago.

"Are you finished?" I ask.

She folds her arms over her chest in a huff. "No, but I'm sure you're going to interrupt me to spew your lies."

"No, I'm going to interrupt you to remind you of an agreement we made a long time ago."

Her wheels start turning as I speak. "We were five when we made that deal! You can't hold me to that now."

"We've kept every other promise we've made. We lie, but we keep our promises."

She rolls her eyes. "I promised to hunt. You promised to kill for me. And if either of us failed, then—"

"Then, we owed the other anything we wanted—and I want you."

You might think the promise was something silly little kids promise each other—like play getting married or promising to never give each other cooties.

That might be what it was for Liesel. She hunted down a spider in her room, but couldn't go through with killing it. So she called me. I promised to always kill for her. She promised to hunt down any creature.

It may have started as innocent kids making silly promises. But for me, it was so much more. We promised each other a life if we failed. And we've both failed more times than we can count.

I'm ready for my life.

I'm ready to end this.

I'm ready to learn her truths while keeping my lies.

I'm ready to win and take the truth of that moment, along with hundreds of others to my grave.

Liesel will never know my truth, but before the end of this year, I'll learn hers.

I watch Liesel closely as she realizes what's happening.

"You're really going to use a promise that we made when we were kids to get me to go with you? To take me as your prisoner? To convince me to follow you? To become your slave? To let you own me?" Her voice gets louder with each question.

I'm silent.

She knows I'll use whatever I can against her to get her to come with me. She can either come willingly, or I'll take her. She can't keep running and hiding.

Her chest rises and falls quickly under her stained sweatshirt. She's considering her options and realizes she has none. She needs answers as much as I do.

We both need answers.

We both need truths.

We need to continue to hide behind our lies until the bitter end.

What happened that day when we were five changed the course of both of our lives and led us here.

"What will it be, Liesel? Will you come with me willingly, or will I take what is owed to me?"

She shakes her head slowly. "You evil bastard. You have no right to take me. I'm not yours. I'm not your property!"

"I'll take that as a no, you won't come willingly."

"I will fight tooth and nail. And I will never stop fighting. You know my past. You know the pain I've endured. You will never break me. You will never get any truths from me."

"I know."

"Then what do you want with me? My body? To fuck me every night like your whore?"

I'm silent.

"You want my money? My power? My name?"

I don't answer her. I let her throw her theories out. I let her spill her lies. I let her expel her anger out. Better to get it out now than later.

"What do you want with me?" she yells.

I step closer, and to my surprise, this time, she doesn't back away. She's done running. She's ready to fight. I'm prepared for her to draw a knife, a gun, even blow up the entire house with both of us in it if she has to. I knew she would fight when she was done running. It's exactly what I want.

I grab her wrist and yank her to me until my breath is just above her mouth. I pause, lingering for my words to make the most impact.

"I want the same thing I've always wanted—I want to know what was on your half of the paper. I want to know the truth, not the lies. I want the treasure that secret leads to. I want to take everything from you. I want the truth, Liesel, and I don't care what I have to do to get it."

"Why do you want the treasure? You have more money than you could possibly ever need."

"To ruin you." *Like you ruined me.*

"You won't kill me," she says, her voice shaking, not sure if her words are true or more lies.

"If killing you gets me the secret, I will."

Then I shove a sleeping pill into her parted lips and cover her nose and mouth with my hand.

She struggles for a moment as she backs into the corner of the wall. Her eyes go big, and the veins in her eyes turn bright red as she struggles for breath but still refuses to swallow the pill.

"I'm crueler than you'll ever be, Liesel. You don't know how far I'll go. You may think what I did to Siren was savage, but it is nothing compared to what I will do to you."

She stops fighting as more oxygen leaves her body. Soon she won't have a choice but to surrender.

She closes her eyes hard and then opens them defiantly before finally swallowing. I may win this round, but she thinks she's only allowing me so she can fight another day. So tomorrow she can slice my balls clean from my body.

I kiss her neck, thanking her for swallowing the pill that will soon knock her unconscious.

"I can't wait for you to fight back, Liesel. I'm going to enjoy every second of it. But for now—sleep. Tomorrow you can fight."

I remove my hand, and she gets one solid breath in before she collapses. I catch her in my arms, finally having a moment to really study her. To hold her close. To revel in the fact that she's finally mine.

Mine—if only that were true.

13

LIESEL

Life or death.

How much does Langston know?

Does he know my truth or only part of it?

Does he know the missing piece of the puzzle I've been desperately trying to put together for years?

No, there is no way he knows the truth, but he does have the missing piece of information. There is no way to know its significance without the rest, which is why he needs me.

I hear the roar of the plane engine near my head, giving me a pounding headache.

I want to open my eyes, but I won't, not until I've figured out every clue I can while Langston still thinks I'm asleep.

I'm surprised I'm on a plane. I thought he would take me back to Enzo and Kai's compound to be tortured until I told the truth. Or at the very least back to Langston's house, which is also in Miami.

I'm a monster with plenty of dark savageness in my heart, but it doesn't mean that I deserve to be taken like property.

So why am I on a plane?

Is the plane flying around in circles to confuse me before he inevitably takes me to the dungeons in the Black house? He thinks if I don't know where I am, I'll be more scared. He doesn't know there is only one thing I fear.

One thing in the entire world—and Langston can't use that fear against me.

No one can.

Not anymore.

I smell coffee brewing nearby, and I'm desperate for a drink. It would help my splitting headache from Langston's sedative.

But I doubt Langston will serve me coffee now that I'm his slave.

Dammit.

I'll survive whatever he has planned for me. I'm more than strong enough. I'm a survivor.

But that doesn't mean I'm happy about it.

In the end, Langston will pay with his life for what he's about to do to me.

He thinks fucking me against my will will bring back all the horrible memories from that night. It will make me talk. That he won't even have to actually fuck me to get me talking, just threaten me with rape.

I smirk. He doesn't know me at all—not anymore.

"You can open your eyes. I already know you're awake," Langston says.

"Why? So I can look at your ugly face? No, thank you."

Langston sighs. "Get up, Liesel. Don't make this difficult."

"I'm not going to listen to a word you say. I'm going to make this as difficult for you as possible."

Then the bastard puts the cup of coffee right under my nose. It's a heavenly smell and my parched mouth waters. I'm desperate for a taste. My body betrays me and opens my eyes, showing how desperate I am for the cup of coffee.

I reach for the cup—he jerks it away just out of reach.

I grit my teeth together to keep my steaming anger inside. I feel the burning anger in the pit up my stomach shoot up my chest like lava, but I won't let it gush all over him until the right moment. As much as I want to tell him off right now, I don't have any power on a private jet miles over the ocean.

I sit up on the couch and lean my head back against the wall.

Only then does Langston hold the cup out to me again.

I don't immediately reach for it this time. I just watch him, trying to figure out the thoughts churning in his head. There was a time when I knew exactly what he was thinking before he spoke it.

"Take it, Liesel."

That only makes me want to disobey more. But damn do I want that coffee. *No, I need it!* It may seem ridiculous, but I know that I need that coffee to survive. I'm going to need every bit of my strength, every drop of caffeine to fuel me.

I snatch the cup out of Langston's hand and drink it before I feel any self-pity that makes me want to throw the cup of coffee in Langston's face.

The coffee tastes like heaven to my dusty mouth. It's warm and rich with a hint of cherry and chocolate—my favorite.

I look up at Langston, expecting him to gloat. To say 'good girl' or something condescending, showing that he's in control instead of me.

Instead, Langston stares at me like he's seeing me for the first time. His eyes have narrowed, his jaw clenched, his mind closed off. I can't tell if he's angry, or happy, or confused, or annoyed, or pissed, or turned on. All I know is there is a lot of emotion brewing beneath the surface of that half scowl, half awe expression.

We sit silently as I drink my coffee. I don't know what's

about to happen next; this might be my only moment of happiness for the day, week, month, year…

So I savor every sip.

Down to the last drop.

Langston stands up just as I'm about to finish my cup and walks to the front of the private plane and disappears through a door, leaving me alone in the back. Some people might try to take this chance to snoop, to find a weapon, something to help me escape.

But that would be a waste of time. Langston is better at wielding a gun than I am. Even if I had a gun or knife, he'd stop me long before I was able to wound him. And there is no escaping on a private jet.

Langston returns a minute later with a pot of coffee and a plate of scones. He snatches the cup from my hand, refills it, then hands it back, before putting two scones on a plate next to me.

He doesn't give me an order, but it's clear in his gaze that he wants me to eat or he'll force-feed me.

My queasy stomach makes my decision easy. Whatever he drugged me with has made my head dizzy and my stomach upset. I need food. I pick up one of the scones and nibble on it.

"Where are we going?"

Langston leans back in his single chair across from me on the couch. He's wearing his usual outfit of jeans, boots, and a plain black T-shirt. He blends in and is ready to fight at a moment's notice.

He looks like Langston, but there is a heaviness to his stare. Something has changed about him; I just can't put my finger on it.

Not that I care. I don't care about Langston. I need to get him out of my life, once and for all.

"You'll find out soon enough."

I sigh. *Same old Langston—it's either no answer or a lie.*

"What are you going to do to me?"

He peers out the window next to him as if he didn't even hear my question. *Or maybe he's considering how to answer me?*

Finally, his heavy gaze returns to me, and I wish he'd kept staring out the window. As much as Langston tries to hide it, there is only one stare he gives me when he looks at me. And as much as I try to hide it, there is only one reaction my body returns when he stares.

Lust.

No matter how we hate each other, we missed our opportunity for one night in the bed, and our bodies resent us both for that.

That's probably why I'm here? For Langston to have his way with me. That way, he gets control of his lust without giving up any power to me.

I'm not naive enough to think I could truly fight him. If he wants to torture me, rape me, kill me, he can. But I can make the memory one that haunts him for the rest of his life.

"If I answer you, you won't believe me," Langston says in a deep octave that vibrates through my chest cavity and hits me in the heart, making it beat rapidly in response.

"That's right, you're a liar."

He smirks. "Same as you."

"How long will you keep me?" He'll hurt me to get whatever he wants—my pain may, in fact, be what he wants. He's a sadistic bastard, after all.

I know what he did to Siren—all in the name of helping her. They are besties now, but she doesn't know him like I do. She doesn't know the true depths of his danger.

"Seatbelt," Langston says suddenly out of nowhere.

I glance out the window and realize we are low to the ground. It looks like we are about to land in the ocean, not on land, but I know that isn't true.

I buckle my seatbelt and stare out the window for clues as to where Langston will hold me captive until he gets whatever he wants from me.

I spot the small island we are about to land on. The water is crystal blue.

Caribbean?

Hawaii?

Maldives?

There are so many places we could be landing. I don't know how long I was unconscious. For all I know, we could just be over in Key West, or we could be thousands of miles from Miami, like the coast of Australia.

Langston won't be telling me the truth, but hopefully, the airport will have signs once we land to tell me where we are.

We approach the rough-looking runway, and I'm glad I put my seatbelt on. The runway looks more dirt than concrete.

I brace myself, and I notice Langston do the same as we make a rough, bumpy landing.

I stare out the window, waiting for a building or other planes to come into view. None do.

The plane slowly creeps to a stop, but no cars drive up to greet us. No security comes to check our passports.

It seems we've landed on an island in the middle of nowhere.

I look over to Langston, who is looking at me curiously with a small grin lifting up his sharp cheeks, like he knows it will piss me off that he took me to a place I'll have trouble escaping.

If there were men here on the island, I could escape. Use my powers of flirtation to get one to help me, but I can't use that power if there are no people.

"Would you like to change, or are you going with the castaway look for our entire trip?" Langston says, his eyes dragging up and down the dirty rags I'm wearing.

I want to change, but he's won enough for one day.

"How long?" I say, my voice tighter.

"Long enough that your boyfriend will get worried. Long enough that he will give up looking for you and find someone else to become the future Mrs. Waylon Rogers."

I shake my head. "Waylon will never stop looking for me."

Langston laughs. "I give him six months tops before he moves on. He's planning on running for office, and he knows that having a beautiful woman on his arm will serve him well."

Beautiful—that's the only characteristic that Langston uses, like beauty is all that matters.

"Don't underestimate him. He has money—more than you do. And we both know that men with money usually get what they want."

Langston unbuckles his seatbelt.

I do the same.

I stand to follow him off the plane.

"How long?" I repeat again. He won't give me any other answers, but I need to know how long I have to endure whatever he has planned. It will give me something to focus on.

Langston mentions six months, but that was just a random number he threw out to frighten me. I doubt Langston has six months to give up with me on this island. He works for Kai and Enzo Black. He's part of their family—basically, a brother to Enzo and Zeke. They won't let him hideaway on an island with me for long. They will say I'm a lost cause, and he should give up whatever he thinks he's going to accomplish with me.

Langston whips around at my words. "I told you I

wouldn't answer you. No matter what my answer is, you won't believe it anyway."

"One month? Two? Three? How long?" I ask, watching the vein on his forehead balloon as he becomes more impatient with my annoying question.

Then he turns and walks toward the plane's door to exit.

I realize there is no one on the plane except the pilot.

"If you're going to rape me, just get it over with tonight. Rape me all week, and then we can both go home next weekend," I mumble under my breath.

That does it.

Langston snaps.

Turning on a dime, he has my arms pinned above my head, my body pressed against one of the windows, and my pelvis pinned with his.

He's breathing hard and fast—out of control. His eyes shine red, his nostrils flare, and the demon within him comes out to play.

He might rape me right here, right now.

Good—get it over with.

"Why would I give you what you want? Why rape you today when I can take my time? When I can make you wait and fill your head with all the torturous things I will do to you?"

"Because then you would have to wait too. You're the most impatient man I've ever met. You *can't* wait."

He grips my wrist with one hand as he strokes the side of my face with his knuckles so gently. The combination of his rough grip combined with his soft touch sends delicious sinful desire through my body.

I hate men being rough with me. *So why does his grip turn me on, even a little bit?*

"I've waited a long time for this, Liesel. I think I can wait a bit more."

"How long?" I breathe, my voice giving away my neediness.

"As long as it takes."

Langston releases me and undoes the door of the plane, leaving me with his parting words.

As long as it takes.

As long as it takes for what?

Langston stops just before he exits the plane and pulls out his gun. He aims it into the cockpit. "But this only ends one way—"

He fires.

I scream.

I don't have to look to know that he shot the pilot.

"Death."

14

LANGSTON

I don't mean she's going to stab me in the heart with a knife or shoot me in the head with a gun—no, I mean she's going to kill me slowly with her luscious lips, her sparkling eyes, her deadly curves. She's going to break me down by throwing her alluring body at me and her smart mouth until I give in and spill everything I know.

We both share a secret.

One from when we were children.

I have half of the secret. She has the other.

Neither of us can do anything with the information we have without the other.

But neither of us is willing to share the truth because we don't want the other to have any power over the other. Once the secret is shared, it will be a battle to solve the puzzle that will lead to the changing of our lives forever.

I used to think that we would never solve the puzzle, never share the secrets. But things have changed, and we no longer have a choice. Time is no longer on our sides.

Liesel doesn't realize this yet, but she will. She may want

to hide the truth, but she doesn't know that time is running out every day.

I hear Liesel climbing down the stairs of the plane behind me as I walk across the dirt runway. I'm not worried about her running off; there is nowhere for her to run off to. That's why I chose this island.

I throw a glance over my shoulder anyway, to see what she will do once her feet hit the ground. She thinks I'll rape her, torture her—she's not wrong. I'll do anything it takes to get the truth.

Anything.

That's how badly I need her to share her secret.

Liesel is right to think I'll hurt her. She's only ever seen the worst of me. The worst of me is harsher than the devil himself. I've killed more men than Enzo or Zeke combined.

Tortured more people.

Ruined more lives.

You could blame my rough childhood on why I am the way I am, but I don't. I blame no one. I chose this life. I wanted this life.

Liesel thinks she's seen the worst of me, but I'm capable of so much more.

Most women would run in a situation like this. Run, flee, hide somewhere on the island to avoid being hurt. Others might search the island for any civilization to help her.

Not Liesel.

She knows the truth of her options. She knows she can run, but she'll only end up dead from dehydration. She knows that anyone she finds on the island works for me.

She's right on all accounts.

The only way off this island is death or me.

For now, I'm the lesser of two evils.

Her last option is to fight.

That's the option she'll choose, but she will take her time

—planning, scouting her options until she knows everything there is to know about the island. Until she thinks I've lowered my defenses. Then she'll strike.

I'll be ready, though.

Liesel will follow me wherever I go for the time being. She will want to learn everything she can. So I don't have to worry about giving her orders or tying her up. Not yet.

The island is split in two. One half holds a small native population of maybe a hundred people. The other half is vast jungle forest, almost completely uninhabited, except for one house—the house I own.

I could call a car and we would be at the house in ten minutes, *but where's the fun in that?*

So instead, I throw my backpack over my shoulder, carrying the essentials—water, food, a change of clothes. And then I take off into the jungle.

"Really, Langston? You don't have a car, a four-wheeler, something, to take us to wherever we are staying?" Liesel shouts.

I smirk. Liesel pretends she's a girly girl—one who is afraid to chip her nails or mess her hair or makeup up, but that's not who she really is. At least, that's not who she used to be.

"I would call for one if there was a car to call on the island," I lie.

Her feet stop moving. I no longer hear the crunch of leaves under her feet. "There isn't anyone else on the island?"

"Just the two of us."

Her mouth falls open as she stares back at the plane—the only chance she had to escape is now gone after I shot into the cockpit.

"We're really alone?" she asks, recomposing herself.

"Yes."

She grips her oversized sweatshirt around the neck, tightening the garment against her body like she's hugging herself. She's going to sweat to death in that sweatshirt. The only benefit is that she might get fewer bug bites this way.

I want her to take it off so I can get a better view of her body; it would make the hike more enjoyable. But I'm not sure my cock would survive if that were the case.

The one thing I know is that I won't be fucking Liesel tonight, not even if she begged. And she won't beg. If I touched her, she'd scream rape. She would survive and keep her secrets locked away.

She's suffered a lot in her past, more than any woman ever should.

My throat closes up, and my eyes water just thinking about what she's endured. It's going to take a lot more than violating her to break her. *A lot more.*

Pain and fear are only one way to get her to the edge of breaking. Something much harder is the only way to get her to fully break. Something so dark and dangerous that I'm not even sure if I can endure it—but we must.

A trek through the woods is going to do little to wear her down. It will irritate her, but it'll be worth it to sleep under the stars with her tonight.

Tomorrow we can sleep in the mansion. Tonight is about getting reacquainted with each other.

She stomps over to me, and the next thing I know, she's pulled her sweatshirt off and tied it around her head to shield her head from the sun. Her sports bra shows off her flat belly just above her sweatpants. She's wearing tennis shoes, so this trek isn't too hard for her. It's not like she's wearing six-inch heels.

"Did you come prepared with any water or gear, if you expect me to hike through the jungle and risk catching malaria? Or are you hoping I'll die of dehydration or become delirious to make it easier for you to rape me?"

I roll my eyes at her rape joke. She thinks that's all this is about—a sexual tension and itch I need to scratch, that I've brought her here to fuck and nothing more. She has no idea of the truth.

I reach into my backpack and pull out a water bottle and sling it at her. She catches it and sips on the water.

"Now, stop complaining and get moving. We have a couple of miles to hike before dark."

"Are we building a house too tonight? Or is there somewhere we are making it to? I'm guessing not since there are no cars on the island."

"I thought we'd sleep under the stars like we did when we were children."

"You better have two tents and two sleeping bags in that small backpack of yours."

I grin. "Nope, just water and some food."

She puts her hands on her hips like she just can't believe she's stuck with my incompetence. "Really? You didn't even pack a tent? I'm not staying out here on this island for days or weeks without at least basic shelter. We are both going to die."

"Stop being dramatic. We aren't going to die. I was a Boy Scout, remember? I know how to survive in the woods for years without anything but a knife. And I have a lot more than a knife on me."

"I don't think your handgun is going to help much with hunting, Langston."

"Maybe you can bore the poor creatures to death with your incessant whining."

"I wouldn't have to whine if you didn't kidnap me and leave us stranded on an uninhabited island!"

I walk through a bush, pushing a branch back hard and then releasing it just as Liesel walks through. She catches it with one hand to avoid it hitting her face.

"Real mature," she says, pushing it back to walk through behind me. When she releases it, though, her hand is bloodied from the thorns on the branch.

"Your hand," I say, holding mine out.

She shakes her head.

"You need to clean it out and bandage it; you wouldn't want to get an infection in the middle of nowhere, would you?"

She glances around, and then a smug smile trickles over her lips. She hikes off the trail I've made and yanks a couple leaves off a nearby bush, then stomps back. She takes her water bottle, pours water over her wounds and applies the leaf to her hand.

"There. This is an aloe vera leaf; it has medicinal powers. No infection."

I study the leaf closer. "Looks like poison ivy to me."

Her eyebrows jump up, and she goes to remove the leaves, but my heavy chuckle stops her.

"I hate you."

I snicker. "Right back at you."

She stomps past me deciding to take the lead, which is fine by me. I can enjoy her ass so much better from this angle. But I do end up having to duck a lot to avoid branches hitting me.

"And as for your kidnapping comment—I didn't kidnap you, just held you to an arrangement we had."

She huffs, jumping over a fallen tree trunk. "One we made when we were five. I don't think that counts. This is kidnapping, and as soon as I get back to the mainland, I'll make sure you are punished for everything you do to me."

I look at her with a dark expression. "I didn't think you were patient enough to wait to punish me until we get back."

"You're right, I should punish you sooner."

"It's getting dark; we should find a spot to sleep for the night."

Liesel wipes the sweat from her brow, and I know she's relieved to not have to walk any further tonight.

We are maybe twenty minutes or less from the house with air conditioning, a nice bed, a shower—all the things Liesel craves.

But I'm the cruel bastard who is going to make her sleep in the dirt, in the heat, with mosquitos swarming.

"Start collecting firewood, I'll work on the fire," she says.

I like it when she's bossy, but it doesn't mean I'm going to let her be in control. "Do you remember how to start a fire? I'm guessing you haven't been camping since we were kids?"

"I can start a fire—just get the wood."

I hold back a smile as I collect wood and underbrush to start a fire. As warm as it is now, the first rule of camping under the stars is having a fire. Nights can get cold, and it will keep any wild animals from coming too close.

I pull out another water bottle to drink and sit on a fallen tree as I watch Liesel struggle with the fire. She tries over and over again, getting more and more frustrated.

She's covered in dirt, sweat, and mosquito bites. Finally, she falls back to the ground, exhausted.

"You win, again."

I stand and flick a lighter into the woodpile. It starts up immediately.

"That's cheating," she looks at the fire, still lying on her back, her breasts pushed up in her bra, revealing more of her stomach.

I could stare at her all night. She's beautiful even though she's covered in mud and dirt. Her body calls to me—begging me to show her how to truly fuck. That little show she put on for me with her boyfriend wasn't fucking. She doesn't know the meaning of the word.

I could show her.

My mind spins with thoughts of how I could take her here on the dirt, against the tree, or in the ocean.

"Are you okay? You look like you're about to go murder an innocent rabbit for our food," she says.

I reach into my backpack, pull out two Snickers bars. I toss her one and keep the other for myself.

"I won't be hunting for rabbits tonight. I'd rather hunt for something else."

She's halfway opening the wrapper, when my words catch her by surprise. She freezes and looks at me, searching for answers behind my words. I'm not going to make this easy for her.

I had to kidnap her. And I'll have to go much further to get the info I need from her.

"You have no need to hunt me, you already got me. Or do you think I'll run off in the night?"

I take a bite of my bar. "You can run, but we both know no matter where you go on this island, I'll find you. You can't hide from me. And if I don't find you, dehydration or exhaustion will."

She continues to lie on her back as she nibbles on the corner of her bar, savoring every bite. She doesn't know I have a dozen more in my backpack. She thinks this might be her only meal I give her.

Torturing her by withholding food or water isn't really the best method to get her to talk to me. No, what I have planned is more sinister and won't require me to watch her wither away into bones.

I like her curves. I want her curves. I'm a selfish asshole in that way. I won't mark her body in any permanent way. I can't say the same about her soul.

I wait until she's finished with her bar before I speak again.

And wait.

And wait.

And wait.

I'm not a patient man, but I'm becoming one with her. The more patient I am, the more I mess with her head, the higher the chance she will start talking.

The sky has turned to dusk. The moon has started peeking out behind the trees, shining down on us. The fire illuminates her silhouette casting shadows over her face.

"Why did Fitz write you a threatening letter? Why did he want to kill you?" I ask.

I already know the answer.

Liesel knows the answer too.

This is a test of trust and truth. *Will she answer me honestly? Or will she lie?*

"I don't know. I'm as bewildered as you are. I would guess Waylon's first political run put a target on us. Fitz wanted our money, and he thought we'd pay to avoid a scandal," Liesel says, pulling her sweatshirt over her chest as she shivers. The wind has picked up, and the fire alone won't be enough to keep her warm tonight. She stares up at the scattered stars through the trees, not looking at me.

Lies it is.

She didn't tell me the truth. She knows why Fitz came after her. It's the same reason I came after her—to figure out her secret and find the treasure she's hiding.

My heart thumps hard like the beat of a war drum picking up steam. I used to like the lies we shared. Not anymore. There is too much at stake.

Liesel looks over at me, either because she can hear the heavy beat of my heart or because she wants to see my reaction to her lie.

Her lips thin as she tries to hide her emotions, but I can

tell I've lit a spark of fear in her. I look like a deranged madman and the possibilities of what I will do scare her.

"No more lies, Liesel."

She sits up, tucking her knees to her chest as she tries to stay warm on the opposite side of the fire from me.

"We don't know how to do anything else, Langston. Don't pretend like you've told me the truth either. I'm not here because of some silly promise when we were five. I'm not here because I owe you for killing Fitz. I'm here because of that damn letter you ripped in two.

"Nothing has changed, though. I won't tell you what my half said, and you won't tell me what your half said. So why try to get answers now? Why am I here?"

She hasn't earned the truth. She hasn't earned an answer. But I'm about to give her more truth than she'll get from me the rest of her time here.

"I want the truth. And I will get the truth—no matter what it takes. The sooner you tell me everything you know, the better for you.

"Let's start with one. One truth you've never told another soul. One piece of yourself that has only ever belonged to you."

The wind stops. The leaves stop rustling. It's eerily quiet as my words are the only sound on the island.

"I tell you a truth, and I go free?" she asks, her voice pained. She'd rather be raped, tortured; her body pulled apart limb by limb than offer me a truth. She will never admit that to me, but it's true.

I shake my head. "One truth buys you more time on this planet. A lie shortens my patience, resulting in less time."

"That gives me no incentive to tell you anything!"

I gave her a path to freedom. *Death is freedom, right?*

For most people, one honest truth would be easy. Not for Liesel. Not for me. Not when your whole life has been a lie.

She takes a deep, exhausting breath—one that consumes her whole body, and then as she exhales a breath so strong it persuades the winds to pick up again. And then she looks to me like a scared little girl.

I try to squeeze out the thoughts of the girl I used to know. The one wearing pigtails and pretty pink dresses, who would run through the forest and chase after me and our boy crew. She was the princess we all protected. We all failed.

She was the one that got away.

Not anymore.

Now, she's mine. I have her trapped physically, but I need more.

"So what will it be? Ready to tell the truth and earn more time? Or lie and be punished?" My voice is deep and haunting. She has no idea why I'm pissed—what she did that makes me so willing to hurt her, kill her. She never will. But she knows that I'm serious when I say that I will hurt her if she doesn't tell the truth.

She nods as she shakes out her hands, but I can see them trembling. She's trying to psych herself up to speak—to tell the truth.

"I'll tell you a truth, and for every truth I tell you, I'll be the one hurting you. I'll kill you with truths."

Liesel means every word she says. I have no doubt that she will choose whatever vicious truths she can come up with to hurt me. To cut me down until I beg her to stop.

However, the only things that could hurt me are her lies.

15

LIESEL

Langston wants a truth.

There are so many truths to choose from. So many from my past that frighten me, including one that I'm afraid will change the course of my life forever.

I'd rather him rape or torture me than make me tell the truth. I'd do anything to avoid my past.

Langston knows that better than anyone.

As much as I'm all talk, telling him to rape me and get it over with, I don't want him to hurt me. I'll do anything to avoid being hurt by Langston, because I remember the boy I used to care about, buried beneath his brawny exterior. Knowing that boy grew up to be a true killer is more than I can stand.

So I'll try to tell the truth. I'll try to gain more time. I'll try to hunt for my freedom and hope that Langston doesn't kill me.

An idea forms as I sit across the fire. I tremble from a combination of the cold and my fear. If it keeps me safe from Langston, then I'll do almost anything to make that happen.

Langston is being relatively nice at the moment, but there

is nothing he isn't capable of. The darkness in his heart rivals my own. Everyone may think I got out, that I'm no longer mixed up in the underworld, but they don't know all the horrible things I've done since.

Langston is the same. And right now, I'm his prey.

I won't let him hurt me.

He's sitting on a log across from me. He thinks he's more powerful sitting higher than me, but he just gave me the ammunition to fire back and win.

"The first night I was raped…" I start.

"Telling me about your rapes won't earn you your freedom, but if you want a free counseling session, be my guest. I'll enjoy listening to all the ways you were abused. It will give me lots of ideas on how to break you."

His words are harsh and villainous. I just wish I knew if they were true or not. His words are meant to strike fear into me, but there is nothing physical he could do to me that would make me tremble quite as much as I am now.

"Will you shut up? You want a truth, then let me tell the story."

"One more thing," he says.

"You don't get to add addendums to our deal now."

He leans forward, closer to the fire, and the flames reflect in his eyes as if the fire is coming from his eyes, not the pit.

I gasp at the evil I see reflected back at me.

"You aren't in control, huntress. You never were. You are lucky I'm giving you a way out at all. I could just torture the truth out of you and then kill you. That would be easier."

"You would never kill me," I call out his lie.

"Things have changed. You aren't someone I care about anymore. The Liesel I once knew is gone."

"That she is," I agree, my voice stronger than I feel.

"If you lie, instead of telling me the truth, if you tell a truth you've already told before, I will punish you."

"You'll punish me if I'm silent."

His eyes disappear back into the darkness, but I know my words are true. It doesn't matter. He'll hurt me, drive fear into me, all so that he can get power over me. He may say he's only hurting me to get info, but he'll enjoy every second of it.

"Continue with your story if you dare, but know what awaits you if you lie."

I want to move closer before I open my mouth. I want to be able to read all of his expressions. But I dare not move closer. If I move at all, I'll lose my resolve and won't tell my story.

No, I won't let the fear win. I haven't been afraid of anything in years. I won't start now.

I stand up. I won't move closer to Langston, but I'll stand taller as I speak. I have power. I have strength. And this story is the start of that.

"The night I was raped should have been the worst night of my life," I start again, wishing the wind would pick up again to drown out my voice. Instead, it's stopped, ushering in an eerie silence, as if the entire forest is listening to my story, ready to call me a liar if I slip one time.

The quiet pushes my thoughts back to the beginning, back to the moment fear became normal in my life—the moment when I learned how evil men could truly be.

It's not the story I intended to tell. This part of the story Langston already knows, but it's what spills. I become consumed, and I can't do anything but speak what happened…

———

I finally bought my first bikini, even though I'd asked my mother for one every year for the last three years. I finally saved up enough money to buy one from hours working at the ice cream shop.

I could have just asked Enzo for the money, and he would have gladly given it to me. Enzo doesn't need to worry about something as simple as money. He doesn't have to save and scrap. He just has it, an overabundance of it.

He's not in the pool yet, but I know he normally swims around this time, so I start doing laps myself. I hear a splash and look up to find Enzo swimming towards me.

I watch Enzo's arms stretch over his head and dip into the water. His muscles lengthen and contract as his legs propel him forward. He could swim laps for hours without stopping to rest. He's a machine.

Soon, he'll be mine.

"Enzo," I shout, excited to see him.

He stops mid-stroke and turns in my direction.

It takes everything in me to not drool or let my mouth hang open at the sight of him shirtless. I've watched him swim countless times, and each time I'm shocked by how sculpted he is. How his muscles look like they've been chiseled by an artist into his chest—they are too perfect to have been gained from just regular working out. And that happy trail that leads down into his black swim trunks—yummy.

"Do you need something, Liesel?"

I walk up the shallow stairs, so he can see my body, and put my hand on my hip. When I shift my weight, he notices. His eyes heat, wanting to touch my hip.

I'm elated, but I try to keep my face sultry and indifferent.

"Want to join me for a swim?" I try to let my voice drop, to show how mature I am.

I've been infatuated with Enzo since my mom got a job here when I was ten. My interest in him has only grown as we've both grown older. Enzo is the boy for me. He's the strongest boy I know. He would never hurt me. He is powerful enough to protect me. Someday he'll own the Black empire—the money, the houses, the yachts—all his. And he's smoking hot. I could fall in love with him.

I want him to be my first.

I've already given away my first kiss, but he could be the one to take my virginity.

Enzo grins smugly as he swims closer to me. I think for a moment that he might be getting out.

I don't really want to swim—I just want an excuse to be half-naked with Enzo.

He walks into the shallow end, towards me. Then I feel him grab my hips.

"Enzo!" I squeal as he pulls me deeper into the pool. I fall headfirst on top of him. He doesn't let go once we are in the water. His grip on my body tightens as if promising to protect me no matter what happens.

We both surface at the same time—gasping for air and laughing as I splash Enzo for pulling me under like that.

"Hold still," Enzo suddenly says as he looks at my face with concern.

I still, except for my heart—it thumps and thumps and thumps, beating in anticipation of what Enzo is going to do.

He's holding me by the waist to keep me afloat in the water, where he's just tall enough to stand.

Enzo's face turns serious. His lips part. He's going to kiss me.

His hands inch up my body painfully slowly. I want him to take his time. I want this moment to last forever, but I'm not sure my heart can survive this slow pace. I need his lips on me like I need air.

His lips against mine might send my heart pounding at the speed of light. I'm not sure I'd survive his kiss, but I'll gladly chance it to taste him.

Finally, his hands are gripping my face.

This is it.

The moment he's finally going to kiss me.

Then, his thumb brushes across my cheek.

"There, you had mascara under your eye." He smiles down at me.

I bite my lip in frustration. *How could he not kiss me?* We are so close.

He's still gripping my face even though my mascara is fixed. We are still inches from each other. My hands are gripping his biceps to keep myself afloat.

I'm not going to miss my shot.

Without thinking, I pull Enzo to me and steal a kiss.

This could ruin everything if Enzo doesn't feel the same way as I do. He could turn me down. He could stay away from me for fear that I will kiss him again.

The second our lips touch, though, I know I have nothing to worry about. A burning desire sparks deep in my belly. Enzo pulls me tighter to him, deepening the kiss instead of pushing me away. I feel how hard he is as his tongue explores my mouth. He's a good kisser, real good.

I feel myself flying high on adrenaline and lust, the longer the kiss lasts.

I want Enzo.

I want his kisses.

I want his body.

I want his heart.

I want him to be mine.

Suddenly, Enzo pulls away. His ears perk up, and he presses a finger to my lips to keep me from talking.

I listen carefully, not sure what we are listening to. Even through my blissful haze, I can make out the car horn as Mr. Black's Bentley locks.

Enzo's father is a horrible man. I know to stay clear of him.

He's cruel and vicious and rules every room he enters. I don't fully understand Enzo and his father's relationship, but I do know that Enzo has no choice but to follow his father's orders.

"Run," Enzo says with intensity in his voice, along with what must be fear.

I don't know why he wants me to run. My only guess is that he doesn't want us to get caught together. His father wouldn't approve of his son, who is about to gain an evil empire, ruling it with a poor maid's daughter.

He boosts me out of the pool and then jumps out next. I start running toward the guest house I share with my mother at the back of the property, even though it kills me to be running from Enzo. But before I take two steps in that direction, Enzo grabs me and yanks me to him, stealing one last hungry kiss.

A kiss that will be my downfall.

"Enzo!" Mr. Black yells from the deck above us.

Goosebumps form and the hairs on my arms rise at the single word.

"Coming, Father." Enzo grabs my arms around my biceps and motions to the basement door nearby.

"Go hide in my bedroom. I'll come find you when I'm done with my father," he whispers.

I nod, speechless. Enzo isn't done with me. He wants more. A tiny thrill shoots through me.

He winks at me before he runs up the stairs to meet his father.

I wait until they've both headed inside before I slip through the sliding glass door. I've done this hundreds of times before, but usually to hang out with Enzo, Zeke, and Langston. Never just Enzo alone.

A grin stretches through my entire body as I race up the back staircase to Enzo's bedroom. I run so hard that I don't notice someone is watching me. Someone is standing in the hallway just outside Enzo's bedroom.

I run smack into his chest.

Only when I look up does my smile vanish.

Enzo isn't the chest I ran into. It's his father.

"Hi, Mr. Black. I, uh…, I was looking for Enzo. We have a school project that we have to work on together. I was just looking for him to see what time we should meet. Is he in his bedroom? Or is he upstairs?"

Mr. Black looks at me with a stern expression. His eyes are thin slits, his nostrils spread, and his mouth tightens.

"Don't lie to me, girl." His eyes run down the length of my body. "You aren't studying looking like that."

I instinctively move my hands over my body to hide it from his gaze. But I'm wearing a tiny red bikini, and I don't have a towel. I've been dripping water all over the hardwood in the hallway.

"I'm sorry. I'll just go." I turn to head back out, hoping like hell he doesn't take my indiscretion out on my mother. I hope he doesn't fire her, thinking that it's the best way to keep me from Enzo.

As I turn, I hear him speak a low command. "Stop."

I don't know why I stop. I just do. My feet seem to stop midair like I just ran into a wall.

"Good girl." He steps closer until I feel his hot breath on my neck. "You're a very obedient girl, aren't you?"

My mouth runs dry. The mouth that was just kissed by a boy I've dreamt about for years, that thought my life couldn't get any better, is now dry and speechless.

I nod, it feels like the right thing to do.

"Liesel?" Enzo asks quietly from up the stairs.

I open my mouth to answer, but Mr. Black grabs my neck. "Don't speak."

There is no threat at the end. Just a command. But with

his hand on my neck, I don't have to know what he will do if I speak.

Mr. Black drags me by the neck into his son's bedroom, still gripping my neck so hard that I'm not sure I'm going to be able to breathe much longer. He leaves the door cracked.

"Liese—" Enzo stops dead in his tracks when he sees his father through the crack in the door. The room is dark, so I have no idea if he can see me or not.

"I told you to go the club and handle business," Mr. Black says demandingly.

"I'm headed there right now."

"See that you do."

Enzo turns. His eyes leave the room. He looks straight at me, and my heart freezes again.

Enzo sees me. He has to.

Do something.

Stop this.

Save me.

I beg Enzo to do something, anything. Just don't leave me here alone.

The seconds creep by in extremely slow motion. But a second later, Enzo turns, and he's gone.

Enzo's gone.

I'm alone.

With his father.

In Enzo's bedroom.

"Good girl," Mr. Black says, loosening his grip on my neck.

I still don't speak, though. I've grown up poor. I know what my mother does to earn extra money, and I know how evil this man is who is holding my neck.

I can see in his eyes what he wants to do with me.

Enzo is gone.

The house is empty.

There is no one to save me.

He'll rape me. Torture me. Kill me if he wants to.

For a split second, I think about fighting back, *but what can I do really?* I have no muscles. I can't get free. If I yell, no one will come.

So I do nothing.

I surrender, hoping it will be over faster, that it will hurt less if I give in.

"Good girl," he says again, watching me silently crumble before him.

I must blackout.

Or maybe my brain blocks it out.

The rest comes in flashes.

My bikini being ripped apart.

Him palming my breasts.

Shoving fingers inside me.

Grabbing my throat so hard it left marks.

Beating me so hard I can still feel the bruises.

Forcing my mouth open to suck him.

Being tied up so hard it left marks on my wrists.

And the violation.

Over.

And over.

And over.

That day was both the longest and the shortest of my life.

In the moment, it seemed to last forever, but huge chunks of the night have been taken from my memory that it makes the day feel too short.

———

Slowly, I start coming back to reality, realizing that I'm not in Enzo's room. I'm in the woods with Langston.

The part of the story I've spoken so far is known. I could

keep going; I could get to the part that he still knows, but if I take it far enough, I could speak a truth he doesn't know.

But I can't.

I'm drained from telling that much of the story.

The pain that comes after is too much. It's not something I speak about.

I won't be able to gain myself more time. I'll be sleeping in the dirt on an uninhabited island with my enemy, who will punish me for lying.

At least I can lash out at him with the end of my story.

I glance over at Langston. He's still sitting on the log; his eyes focused on me through the flames of the fire. He's motionless, expressionless—almost like a statue.

He doesn't speak. He doesn't rush me. He doesn't call out any part as a lie. He doesn't tell me that I've already told this story before.

My eyes meet his for the first time since I've been talking. Actually, I have no idea if my eyes have met his or not. When I was telling the story, it was like I was reliving it.

Now, though, is about delivering a blow to Langston.

"I was angry at Enzo when I thought he knew what happened to me and didn't stop it. When he didn't help me. Didn't save me. But I still wanted him. Still thought I could fall in love with him. He was still the better man, the better choice."

I pause.

And I notice Langston's shoulders tense—disagreeing with me.

"You know why? Because Enzo didn't know what his father did. I just thought he did. He should have known, but he didn't. But there was someone who did know. Someone who watched it all happen from the security camera."

I glare at Langston.

"You. You watched me get raped by that sadistic devil.

You watched my life be torn apart. You saw what happened next, and you did nothing."

My voice shakes as I speak. This isn't new. I've told this story to our friend group. Langston was there. But I've never screamed it in his face. Never confronted him with what could be the truth.

Langston is always watching. He's the best at security. He knew what happened to me. He was either watching in real-time, or he watched a recording.

He knew, and he did nothing.

My body shakes, but tears never come. I don't feel sadness, pain, or fear. Not after that night. Not after my worst night, still yet to come.

Langston watches me through the fire.

And for a moment, I think he's going to say nothing.

"I was just doing my job," he says.

"You're a heartless monster."

He stands up. "And you're a liar."

16

LANGSTON

Liesel is a liar.

A schemer.

She knows how to draw men in with her words. She knows exactly what she's doing. She chose her story well and spun the web of lies so tightly that it's hard to make out which parts are the truths and which parts are the lies.

It pisses me off. I should be able to tell. I know practically everything there is to know about this woman—except for one missing piece. A piece she will eventually tell me, but not without a fight.

She won't fight with her fists. She'll fight with lies. Cruel, merciless lies that will be carved into my heart forever. There is no way to verify which parts are true and which parts aren't.

But I know she lied.

I can verify at least one part of her story that isn't true. And the fact that she didn't fight me when I called her a liar tells me she did indeed lie.

But how much of it was a lie?

I march through the darkness away from the fire, away from her. If I stay, I'll do something I'll regret.

I start jogging as my eyes adjust to the darkness. Working for Enzo and Kai has trained me to see through the jet black night, but it's still careless. I shouldn't leave Liesel alone. I shouldn't run when one wrong step could mean I fall off a cliff or get attacked by a wild animal.

I run from Liesel, but it's more like I'm running from her words. *God, how her words cut me deep.*

It hurts.

It all hurts.

Liesel blames me for the rape, just like she blames Enzo.

I should have been there for her. I should have saved her just like Enzo should have.

But I wasn't watching her on the security cameras. I didn't know. At the time, I was in charge of security at the clubs, not at the house. I was good at hacking back then, but the cameras at the house were the most sophisticated we had. I'm not even sure if I was capable of hacking the system to watch out for her then.

Liesel knows that.

But her words cut me nonetheless. They hurt because despite what she says, I do have a heart—one I've tried to eliminate every chance I've gotten. My life would be much easier if I could. But as hard as I've tried, it's still there.

It just doesn't feel the same way about Liesel as it once did.

All her words rip through me, shredding me to pieces.

The rape.

God, she's told the story before, but hearing it tonight with no one else but us, it hit me harder.

She was just a girl.

We should have protected her.

We failed.

As hard as it was to hear the details again, it was harder to hear of her and Enzo.

How they kissed.

How she wanted him.

Could have loved him.

Maybe even would have ended up with Enzo if it wasn't for his dad.

And I have no idea if it was all a lie or a truth.

She said she forgave him, but could never forgive me.

She shouldn't forgive either of us.

Just like I could never forgive her.

That's what I have to remember when my feelings spike again, being so close with Liesel. I once thought she was the only woman for me. Now, I can't think of a worse human being on the planet.

I stop running, my lungs finally burning, finally reminding me of pain instead of the ache I feel for Liesel after her bearing her story.

"She's a liar, Langston. Don't believe a word out of her mouth," I tell myself as I try to catch my breath.

I put my hands over my head as I walk through the forest.

She's a liar.

Never forget.

As I walk back, the story replays in my head, and I realize that I don't think that was the story she intended to tell, it just spilled out. She didn't have a choice but to speak the words, which makes me think the beginning was true. Everything with Enzo—true. It was the second part she changed to try and hurt me.

I won't let her see my hurt.

My pain.

When I approach the fire where she still sits, I'm stone —emotionless.

"Ready to punish me?" she asks into the darkness. She

can't see me, but she can feel me, just like I can feel the icy daggers she willingly flings in my direction.

I'm silent as I walk back over to my backpack and pull another bottle of water out. I drink it as I sit on the ground, leaning against the log. I stare across the fire at her.

"Rape me just like he did. Ruin me. Make me hate you," she says.

"You already hate me."

She bites her lip. "Do it. Prove to me once and for all— you're the monster I always thought you were."

Provoking me isn't going to work. We both know I'm a monster, but the only way I gain control is if this happens on my terms and not hers.

"Come here," I say.

Her lip slips from her teeth. She thinks I'm calling her bluff, but there is no fear. Liesel isn't afraid of anything. She's lived through hell—there is nothing worse that could happen to her.

Liesel stands and walks to me. She won't fight me, just like she didn't fight Mr. Black. She thinks this is the best way to survive. Get me to rape her, and then she doesn't have to have nightmares about what might happen, she'll already know.

"Sit."

Liesel sits face to face, her eyes turning yellow as the flames reflect off her pupils.

"I didn't bring a blanket. Keep me warm tonight."

She blinks rapidly, her ears straining like she thinks I misspoke.

"What?"

"You heard me."

I lie down on the dirt. I'm not the least bit cold, not after I ran a mile. The fire alone would keep me plenty warm.

But I want her to have to touch me all night. I want her to

feel me. To lose control. To wonder if, at any moment, I might change my mind and have my way with her.

I must break her.

This will drive the first nail in harder than fucking her against the dirt ever would.

"Keep yourself warm," Liesel spits at me.

I shake my head. "You lied. There are consequences. Keep me warm."

"Or?" she asks, wanting to know what I'll do to her if she disobeys.

"There is no 'or.' You will use your body to keep me warm."

We stare at each other—a silent standoff.

The wind howls.

Liesel shudders.

I don't know if she decides to follow my orders or if she's looking to warm herself. Either way, she finally lies down on the dirt next to me.

"Liesel," I warn when she doesn't touch me.

She lifts an arm over my body. It floats in the air, refusing to touch me. It hovers there until her arm trembles, and she can't hold it up any longer. Only then does she let it wrap around my shoulders.

The touch sends a million emotions through us both. It reminds me of when we were kids. Long before she knew Enzo, she knew me. It was my bed she snuck into, not his. It was me she longed for, not him.

"My legs are cold too."

Her eyes shoot up to me, and she practically pouts.

I smirk, but I'm not sure she can see it, which is a shame, because I look irresistible when I smirk.

Her leg moves in a hard lump as she drapes it harshly over my legs.

I close my eyes with a smile. I've formed a tiny, almost

unnoticeable crack in her shell. Tomorrow I'll form another and another. I'll torture her with tiny little cracks until she finally bursts.

I need her truth.

I need her answers.

I need her apology for what she's done.

But I refuse to need her.

17

LIESEL

It's worse than anything Mr. Black did to me.

It's worse than…okay, it's not really as terrible as the worst thing that's ever happened to me, but I imagine this is how it feels to be shot and slowly bleed out to death. Every drop is painful, and you just want to get to the end so it can be over.

Holding Langston feels like that.

I can smell the sweat from his pores that he worked up after he stormed off. It overpowers even the smell of the fire.

I can hear his gentle, controlled breath in and out, louder than the chirp of the bugs and hum of the wind.

I can feel his warmth—there is no way he needs my body to stay warm.

Why do I stay draped over his body, then?

Because as soon as I touch him—I'm his. I can't turn away. Some part of me I thought I had long ago buried likes his smell, how he sounds, his touch. I like it more than I should. I like a man I hate—a man who wants to kill me.

I've always wanted Langston. He was the first boy I ever

133

wanted. I wanted him before I wanted Enzo. I just don't think about that time and wanting Langston was something I never spoke out loud. I never let anyone know, even him.

That could be the truth that frees me, but I will never admit it to Langston.

It was just lust, not want for the man beneath the muscles, the smug smirk, the light-colored hair boy who taught me how to hunt, to search for secrets. He was the boy who taught me to lie.

If I could separate Langston the man from Langston's body, maybe I'd finally give in to my desires, and we'd fuck willingly. Unfortunately, the only way to separate the two is to kill him and then fuck him, and I'm not into necrophilia.

Langston starts snoring. He's asleep. Now's my chance—to break free of his arms, to run.

I don't want to run, but I shouldn't stay snuggled up against him.

I force my head to lift and my arm to slink off his chest.

But his hand grips my arm, gently pulling it back over his chest. He's still snoring; I'm not even sure if he woke up or not.

I huff out a deep breath.

There is no way I'm sleeping tonight.

———

The sun is what wakes me. It's bright and hot and makes me squint as I open my eyes.

I slept.

I didn't think I could.

And I'm still lying on Langston's chest.

I jump up.

"Easy," he says. "Wouldn't want you breaking a nail. There are no salons around here."

I frown as I regain my composure and remember what happened and where I am.

Birds are chirping happily nearby, and I swear I hear monkeys in the distance. We are in the wild, and I just slept on dirt. Well, technically, I slept *on* Langston. I should be grateful, but I'm not.

I fold my arms over my sweatshirt that is once again heating me up. I really should have taken Langston up on his offer for me to wear new clothes. These sweatpants and sweatshirt really aren't made for the jungle.

"What now?" I ask. *Please tell me this was all a joke. That we are in Santorini and he dragged me here to meet Kai and Siren.*

"Breakfast."

He snuffs out the fire and then stretches.

"You have more bars?"

"Nope, you are going hunting for our breakfast."

I laugh. "When you call me huntress, you know it's a nickname, right? I don't actually hunt animals." *I hunt men. I hunt secrets. I hunt truths. Not poor, furry animals.*

"There's a first time for everything."

My stomach growls right on cue, but I refuse.

"I'm not going to hunt and kill an animal. I'd rather starve. I—"

Langston starts walking away even though I haven't finished my sentence.

"Really?" I huff after him, annoyed that he won't even listen to me.

I stop dead in my tracks as Langston pulls something out from behind a tree and holds it out to me.

I blink several times—Langston holds out a bow and arrow.

I scrape my teeth over my bottom lip to hold back my excitement. I haven't held a bow and arrow in my hands since I was ten, when Langston took me "hunting." All we did was target practice since I couldn't kill anything.

I was a perfect shot.

I cautiously reach out for the weapon.

My fingers brush his as I take the bow and arrows in my hands.

I have a weapon.

Something I can use against Langston.

He looks at me wearily. "Don't even think about it."

My eyes light up. "What? I'm not thinking about shooting this arrow into your heart."

He grins. "I'll give you one shot."

"What?"

"One shot to shoot me."

"And what happens when I hit you in the heart and you drop dead? How do I survive?"

He reaches into his back pocket and pulls out his phone. "I unlocked it. When I drop dead, you can call for help."

I lean forward. He unlocked the phone, and it has service.

Langston takes his time walking ten strides away from me. Then he turns and looks me in the eyes.

"I'm waiting."

I hold his gaze as I reach into the bag and pull out a single arrow. It feels familiar in my hand.

I could do this.

I could kill him.

I could...

I take a deep breath as I position the arrow against the bow and pull back on the string, aiming at the ground as I get used to the feel of the bow in my hands again.

And then I look up at Langston—his light blonde hair, his gleaming blue eyes, his tense smirk. He knows that I might shoot him, kill him, but it doesn't matter. Death has never scared him, just like it doesn't scare me. We've seen too much, he and I.

Can I really kill him?

I aim the arrow at his heart.

He doesn't flinch—I doubt even a hurricane sized wind would move him. Langston is testing me, seeing how badly I want to kill him.

I do—I want to be free.

But can Langston really be the first man I kill?

Without another moment to think about it, I let the arrow fly.

The moment the arrow leaves my grasp, I know I've made a mistake.

Was the mistake aiming too high?

Or letting the arrow go in the first place?

My eyes have squeezed shut out of instinct. My heart rattles quickly in my chest as my breath whooshes out of my body at the release of the arrow.

The jungle is still and quiet.

I force my eyes open, terrified to see Langston standing but equally afraid to see him lying on the ground.

Langston.

He's still standing.

The arrow didn't hit him.

I sigh.

"Is that a sigh of relief or a sigh of anguish?" Langston says with a wide grin like we were just playing a game he won—not one that could end in death.

I ignore his snark.

He pulls the arrow from the tree I hit, just over his left shoulder.

"You're rusty," he says as he begins to stride back to me.

I pull another arrow out and aim it at his heart. He's much closer this time. I wouldn't miss a second time.

"Or maybe I missed on purpose, realizing that you were lying, and cell service doesn't work on this barren island."

He takes another step closer until the arrow is touching his chest. Then he grabs it slowly, his eyes begging to be let into a window of my soul.

"Liar."

"Scoundrel."

He grins at that.

"Are you ready to hunt for breakfast now?"

"No." My hands shake at the thought of killing something on this island with my own hands.

He takes the bow from me. "But so sure you would be able to live with killing me."

"You deserve death," I snap back.

He puts the bow and bag of arrows over his shoulder. He looks rugged and woodsman-like, like he could kill any animal that crosses our path. Any human too.

That's Langston—he fits into any situation. The city, countryside, woods, castles. He can belong anywhere.

"Maybe I would have," Langston answers. "But I won't be dying today."

He turns, leaving me no choice but to follow.

I yank my sweatshirt back off and tie it around my waist as I follow Langston pushing through the brush.

"You aren't really going to kill something for our breakfast, are you?"

He looks back at me with an amused expression. "You eat meat, don't you?"

"Actually, I don't," I lie.

"Liar."

I shake my head. "Well, I would be a vegetarian if I had to actually kill the animal before I ate it."

"That I believe." Langston stops, putting his backpack, bow, and arrows down.

"What are you doing?"

"Getting you breakfast without killing anything."

Langston grabs the base of a palm tree and begins to scale it. It takes him five seconds to reach the top. He slices off two coconuts before sliding back down. He cracks them both open and hands me one.

"You're welcome," he says before sucking the juices out.

"Thanks for providing me with food, oh great one. You forget you wouldn't have to feed me if you'd just set me free."

"I could stop providing you with food, then, if you don't appreciate it."

I roll my eyes. "Then I would die from starvation instead of at your hand, before you've had your way with me. Now, who's a liar?"

After that, we finish eating our coconuts without any more smart remarks.

"Let's go," Langston says soon after I've finished my last bite.

"Where? Back to camp?"

He raises a brow with a large smirk as he holds his hand out to me. I reluctantly let him help me off the ground. "No, to my house."

I gasp.

"You're lying."

"Follow me, and you'll find out." He takes off at a quick speed, almost like he's running as he carries his backpack, bow, and arrows.

I run after, still not sure if I believe him or not.

Suddenly, Langston stops at a clearing.

I follow his gaze out to see a large house—the kind you see celebrities renting when they take vacations to private islands. I would guess the house has at least ten bedrooms and as many bathrooms. I can see a large infinity pool, and the landscaping is immaculate. There are people living on this island.

"You son of a bitch! You had us sleep on the ground last night. You made me think that we were on a deserted island, just the two of us. You bastard!"

I hit him squarely in the shoulder. More pissed that he lied to me, tricked me, and I fell for it than I am that he made me sleep on the dirt when there was a mansion with big fluffy beds not ten minutes from where we slept.

He catches my fist before I hit him again.

"We lie to each other, Liesel. Don't expect anything less from me. I will lie, cheat, trick you, hurt you, go as far as it takes. You think what I did last night was cruel? You have no idea what I have planned for you. End this now and tell me the truth."

"I'll decide if I tell a truth or a lie. I'll decide what happens to me."

He stands tall, looking down at me, making hot desire shoot through my body.

Damn him and his commanding expression turning me on.

"You'll tell me every truth you have. You won't be able to survive without spilling your secrets."

I'll survive, alright. He won't get the truth, only lies. I just hope I can keep to my own words. I hope I'm not lying to myself.

18

LANGSTON

I LET Liesel aim an arrow at me, knowing how good of a shot she is. She could have killed me if, deep down, she truly wanted to.

But she didn't. She's not a killer like I am.

She's done some horrible things in her life, but she doesn't kill. Even her worst enemies. *Even me.*

It was a gamble.

I didn't know how Liesel truly felt—now I do. She hasn't changed. She's a monster, done some horrible things. Things she deserves to pay for, die for, but I don't have to worry about her slitting my throat in the middle of the night.

That's where she draws the line—murder.

There are two types of people in this world: the kind who kill and those who can't, no matter the circumstances. You could say there is a third group of people: ones who kill in self-defense, only when their own life is threatened. But those types of people don't exist. It's a lie.

You can either kill or you can't.

It makes no difference the reason why. And once you cross that line, you can never go back.

Liesel hasn't crossed that line. If she can't cross that line to save her own neck now, then she never will.

Still, letting her shoot at me was incredibly reckless.

I shouldn't have been so careless. There was a time when it wouldn't have mattered if I died. Now, it's important to stay alive.

Liesel may not have meant to offer a truth, but she did. It may be the only truth I get from her for a while, but it's a start.

"Stay close," I say to Liesel as we start walking down the hillside toward my home.

She laughs. "I'm not following any of your orders."

She takes off at a full sprint toward the house.

She's not running away. I should just let her throw her tantrum, let her think she's won and punish her for her mistakes later.

But I'm not going to let her gain an inch.

I run after her.

She's quick and has a head start, but I'm faster.

She drops her sweatshirt, trying to sprint faster, but running won't save her.

Two more leaps, and I tackle her to the grass. Liesel tries to fight back, but she doesn't have a chance. I overpower her easily, pinning her arms above her head as my weight holds her waist and legs down. She pants heavily with more anger than fear flickering in her hazel eyes.

She's covered in dirt, sand, and grass. There is nothing sexy about our appearances, and yet my erection pushes against her stomach. There is no hiding it.

I growl instead of claiming her mouth like I want to.

"When I give you an order, you follow it."

She grins. "No. I'm not afraid of you."

"Liar," I breathe against her neck. "I can smell the terror in your sweat, feel the speed of your pulse—you're petrified."

"I'm out of breath from running. Of course, I'm sweating, and my pulse is racing."

I shake my head as I see my staff approaching to greet me. They pause, but Liesel glances up, realizing we have an audience.

"Do you see them?" I say, grabbing her chin and tilting her head up so I know she does.

Her eyes cut back to me.

"They work for me. They know exactly who I am, the evil I've done, and they still choose me. Their loyalty is with me. Every single one would die for me. *Try to turn them. Try to run from them. Try, huntress.*

"Heed my warning…don't trust anyone here. Don't think you are safe. Everyone here has done fucked up things—stolen, tortured, killed. That's the only way they end up working for me. And I won't stop them from hurting you…"

Liesel's eyes widen.

"You are only safe by my side, following my orders. If you do as I say, if you tell the truth, then your life here will be easy."

"I'll still end up dead. What incentive is there to follow your orders?"

I stroke her face, and she turns her head, trying to get away from me.

"Your body might enjoy my touch, but would you enjoy theirs?"

She gasps.

Finally, I got through to her. She's in danger when she's not with me, not following me. It won't keep her from fighting, but it might prevent her from seeking help from someone she shouldn't.

Slowly, I inch off her, despite my body screaming to crush her. To have my way with her right here, right now in the grass in front of everyone. To show everyone that she's mine.

She's not mine. She never will be. Not truly.

I stand, but don't offer her a hand. I watch her closely, waiting to see if she will follow my orders this time or not. When she stands close and doesn't run, she's agreed to be obedient—for now, at least.

I nod my approval at her change in attitude.

It's fake. I'm not naive enough to think this will last, but it will for now.

"Stay close," I say again.

She grabs my hand and squeezes, pressing her vivacious body against mine. "Close enough?" she purrs.

"Don't test me, Liesel."

She lifts our joined hands up to her lips and plants a kiss on the back of my hand. "I'm just doing as you asked."

"Sir, would you like me to take your bag?" Shawn asks.

"Yes, thanks." I realize I dropped my backpack when I was chasing Liesel down the hill.

"Aren't you going to introduce me to your employee?" Liesel asks, batting her eyes like a shy little girl at Shawn.

Liesel isn't shy. This is all an act.

"No, you don't need to know anyone. And they already know who you are."

"Oh? What did you tell them about me?"

"You're a lying bitch, and they shouldn't trust you." I drop her hand.

"At least I'm not a murdering asshole."

I grab her hand again and pull her toward the house. I'm tired of dealing with her smart mouth.

"I'll show you around." The sooner I give her a tour, the sooner I can be done with her. I'll lock her up in a room and run the hell away.

If I spend too much time with her, I'll lose my mind.

"Pool," I say, pointing out the infinity pool that rivals any view in the world. It shoots out over the cliff and looks down at the beach. The sun sets every night over the ocean, and my house has a perfect view.

"Are you just going to state the obvious during this tour or actually point out the things that matter?"

I frown and ignore her, jerking her hand, pulling her along as I walk.

Several of my employees scatter at the sight of us walking in through the back door. *Good, they got the message I made clear to Shawn. Don't talk to us.*

"Kitchen," I point to my left.

"Dinning room," I nod to my right.

Liesel stops, and my arm jerks back. I think she's afraid I'm going to lock her in a dungeon, but when I look at her, I realize she stopped because she's in awe.

She's taking in all the finishings—the bamboo floors, the giant glass doors that open up the entire house, the hand-crafted cabinets.

I take a moment to glance around and really take in the house, trying to see it for the first time through her eyes.

Her mouth falls open when she spots the porch swing that looks like it's in the house, when really it sits just outside the living room. When the glass walls close, the swing is outside, but the doors are almost never closed.

Slowly, her head turns to me. "This house..." she whispers.

She can't finish.

"I didn't build it for you. I built it for me. This was my dream."

One of her eyebrows raises—she's skeptical. She should be. When I built this house, it was built with our childhood dream house in mind. This was the house we both dreamed up when we were nine. This house. Whether I meant to build it for her or for us, it makes no difference. It's our dream house to a T.

"It's incredible," Liesel says, and she really means it.

"I know. I built it. Of course, it's amazing."

That earns me the tiniest smile. For a moment, it feels like we are kids again, teasing each other, instead of foes locked in a battle to the end.

"Let's finish the tour," I say. I don't take her hand this time. I don't want to be connected to her as I realize that sharing this house with her is as personal as if I were to cut my chest open and reveal the depths of my heart.

"This floor is the staff bedrooms," I say, walking her through the house.

The number of bedrooms is the only thing that differs from the house we imagined and this one. In our dream house, we only needed two bedrooms.

One for each of us.

We didn't need bedrooms for staff.

We didn't need bedrooms for kids.

We didn't need guest bedrooms.

In our world, this house was meant to be just ours.

Ours.

Of course, there was never an 'ours,' never an 'us.'

Just her.

And me.

Locked in a bitter war.

I lead her up the stairs.

"More bedrooms," I say, showing her a couple. And then we walk past a door.

"And this room?"

"Is mine, not yours. This half of the house is off-limits to you," I say, pointing down the hallway.

Before she asks more questions, I pull her into my bedroom.

It wasn't my intention to bring her here. I had other plans

for Liesel, but the second I drag her into my bedroom and shut the door, I realize this is where I need her.

Liesel's eyes bulge as she looks around the room, another combination of my and Liesel's dreams. It can turn into a dark cave, like I wanted, at a push of a button—the curtains close, the lights dim, and a dark duvet gets thrown over the bed. But it's also what Liesel envisioned—light, bright, and airy with a picturesque view of the ocean, a balcony for two, and a mostly outdoor bathroom ensuite.

Liesel smiles, really smiles. "You did it. You built our dream. It's beautiful."

I'm silent for a moment.

"It's not yours."

Her smile falters. "I never thought it was."

"You're not going to get free, Liesel. There is no way off this island. You'll live the rest of your life here. You'll die here."

"Then, lucky for me, I'll die in my dream house."

I nod.

She glances out the window, her smile returning. "That is if Waylon doesn't come for me."

"Waylon has money, but no skills. He will never find you. And I doubt he loves you enough to devote his life to searching for you, which is what it would take to find you."

She tucks her mud and leaf-stricken hair behind her ear. "Waylon loves me more than you know. He asked me to marry him."

My throat tightens, and my eyes flatten into slits. I grab her left hand, not believing I missed anything. I hold it up.

"I don't see a ring."

She pulls her hand free. "I don't need a ring for Waylon to prove his love for me. For us to promise to spend our life together forever."

"I don't believe you."

She shrugs. "You don't have to. I'm just trying to warn you. Waylon will come after me. He's not just a fling. He's the only man I've ever loved. And somehow, he feels the same way about me. He loves me. He'd die for me. He won't give up searching for me once he realizes I'm taken."

Liesel is an excellent liar, but it doesn't feel like she's lying now. She has to be. She can't be engaged. She can't want another man. She can't…

"As I recall, you told him you'd be gone for three weeks. So we have at least that long before he suspects anything."

She shakes her head. "He'll expect me to call, to text. We've never gone three weeks without a healthy round of phone sex. You saw how we fucked on the cameras, don't deny it. He'll come looking for me before three weeks."

"That display of sex wasn't love!" I yell in her face.

"How the hell would you know? You haven't ever been in love!"

I open my mouth to scream a truth and stop myself at the last second. I will never admit the truth.

Instead, I grab her arm and pull her into the bathroom.

"Clean yourself off. I'll be back tonight, and you and I will have a little chat about your lying. Until then."

I step back and slam the bathroom door shut, locking her inside.

My blood is boiling. The only person in the world who can drive me this mad is now locked in my bathroom. Those walls won't hold her. If she decides she wants to escape, she can.

The only way to prevent her from running is being with her, but I can't stay here another moment. I need a break. I need to remember why I'm doing this.

Fuck, I need Liesel out of my life for good.

19

LIESEL

IT MAY LOOK like Langston just got the upper hand. I'm locked in his bathroom, after all.

But I won.

I pushed enough buttons that Langston can no longer stand the sight of me. He's losing control already.

He said he's going to kill me, and I believe him.

He said he's learned patience—that I don't believe. If I can get him to lose control, maybe he'll slip, say some hint of his truth or give me a clue of how I can escape.

He ran off instead of laying down the law like he wanted to.

I grin wide.

I'm not going to worry about Langston. Right now, I'm going to enjoy this glorious bathroom—a bathroom I dreamed about when we were kids.

This house only confuses me more. *Why did Langston build the house we dreamed of as kids? Why, if he's hated me this entire time? Wanted me dead?*

So he could torture me with it, that's why.

I won't let him win. I'll enjoy every second of my time in this house, and I won't let him control me.

The entire house is built to enjoy the elements. The bathroom is no different. The shower and tub sit just outside of the main house amongst exotic plants, providing some privacy but allowing you to shower outside while looking at the ocean. There is a freestanding sink attached to the house, and a door that leads to what I assume is the toilet room.

I have my eyes on the shower and tub, trying to choose which one I'm going to use. I suspect Langston will have me locked in here all day, so I decide to shower first to get the muck off, then bathe to soothe my sore muscles.

I step into the glass shower filled with more buttons than a computer after stripping out of my dirty clothes and leaving them in a pile on the bamboo floor.

When I press one of the buttons, the walls slink away into the floor, and then I'm truly showering outside.

I take my time washing, then spend an hour soaking in the tub, letting all thoughts of Langston slip away. Only once an hour has passed of enjoying the ocean, the sun, and the warm, relaxing tub do I let myself think about where I am and what's going to happen next.

I climb out of the bath and look for clothes, but I find none except for the filthy rags that I wore here. I won't be putting those clothes back on.

I find a white robe hanging on the back of the bathroom door and put that on.

Langston wants me to stay locked up like Rapunzel in a tower.

I glance over the edge of the balcony and smile.

Well, he shouldn't have made it so easy for me to escape then.

I'm on the second floor, but jungle vines have grown up most of the balcony.

Without thinking too hard about what I might break if I fall, I hook a leg over the edge and then the other. I hold onto the railing as I try to find my footing.

The sun beats down, making the task harder, as does the robe that I keep stepping on unintentionally.

"Here goes nothing," I say, letting my weight down onto one of the vines.

It holds.

I exhale a deep breath as I start scaling down the vines.

My vine breaks.

I fall, holding onto the vine for dear life, hoping I'll stop.

I do, inches from the ground.

"Holy hell." I laugh, *because what else are you supposed to do when you almost fall to your death?*

I untangle myself from the vine and land on my feet. I retie the robe around me and glance at the house, expecting to see Langston or one of his men chasing after me. This wasn't about escaping; it was about letting Langston know that he loses once again.

I spot the security camera, and I flip it off.

When I glance back through the glass of the house, I don't see anyone coming to chase after me.

Not Langston.

Not his guards.

No one.

I squint at the camera. Langston is watching, surely, but he's allowing me to be free.

Huh.

Still, I don't want to push my luck. I'd prefer to be free as long as I can.

Langston said this island was uninhabited. Obviously, that isn't true, so we must be somewhat close to other houses, businesses, people.

I climb down the cliffside to the beach. There is nothing but beautiful white sand for as far as I can see in either direction.

My feet are already burning in the sand. I wish I had shoes, clothes, something other than this damn robe, but I'll take what I can get. The robe is better than the muddied clothes I had.

So I walk and walk and walk.

I find nothing.

No houses.

No buildings.

No people.

There are obviously people on the island, but they don't live close to Langston. It would take a very long journey to reach another house from here.

And the fact that Langston didn't send anyone after me tells me he's not worried about me running into anyone.

I sludge back to the house as the sun begins to dip toward the water.

Several of Langston's employees are going in and out of the house—cleaning, bringing in supplies, cooking.

"Miss Dunn, I have dinner ready for you. Where would you like to eat it?" a man in jeans and a dark shirt asks me.

I'm surprised he talked to me after Langston made it clear earlier in the day that no one was to talk to me.

"And you are?"

He shakes his head. "I can bring your dinner out to eat on the terrace."

I sigh but nod.

He disappears inside.

I look more carefully at the employees going in and out. They are all muscled, have guns, could be killers themselves. That's why Langston hired them.

"Here you are, Miss Dunn." The man returns with a plate

of food and sets it on the round table at the edge of the terrace.

"Thanks," I say, unsure of myself as he pulls out the chair for me like I'm dining at a five-star restaurant instead of being fed while captive on an island.

He nods, as I sit, and then disappears back inside.

I'm alone again.

I eat my food quickly, realizing I'm hungrier than I thought. I don't taste the food, I inhale it.

I don't know when to expect Langston, but I do know that he's been watching me. He knew the second I would return and had food prepared for me.

So it doesn't surprise me that the second I finish eating, Langston appears.

He doesn't speak or walk loud enough to make his presence known, but my heart recognizes the second he's near.

I look up at him standing in the shadows, just outside the house.

I stare back.

"Did you enjoy your walk?" he asks.

"It was just great, especially knowing there were men watching my every step."

He chuckles. "Up for another walk?"

I tilt my head. "I thought you gave commands, not asked questions."

"I'll be giving orders soon enough. I'll let you decide where we talk tonight."

I stand. "Where do you want to walk?"

"Down to the beach."

I nod.

He picks up a small bag I didn't notice on the floor and slings it over his shoulder, before taking off down the cliffside.

I follow after, still barefoot in my robe.

Langston walks to the edge of the water then plops his bag down. He pulls out a towel and lays it out before sitting down on it. Langston turns and looks at me.

All I see is the glistening water reflecting off the blueness in his eyes. He looks warm and welcoming, not like the killer he is.

He pats a spot on the towel next to him.

I take a deep inhale before sitting down beside him. I'll reserve my strength to fight him later when I'm really going to need it.

Langston gives me a slight nod of approval and then pulls out two lowball glasses.

"Hold," he says, handing them to me.

I take them and hold while he pours two fingers of scotch into each glass. He remembers my favorite drink.

I frown as my eyes slant up to meet his.

"What is this? Why are you being nice?"

He takes his glass and takes a long sip.

"I'm not being nice. This conversation could go long, and I want to be able to enjoy myself while we talk."

I roll my eyes. "Liar. Then why do I get a glass?"

"The drunker you are, the more likely you are to spill the truth and put us both out of our misery."

I down my drink and hold it out with a smug expression.

He shakes his head.

"You don't get more until I say so. We are going for tipsy, not passed out throwing up everywhere drunk."

I pout and continue to hold my glass out to him.

"You look ridiculous," Langston says.

I sigh and set my glass down. "You used to like it."

"Never."

A wave splashes hard against the sand, distracting us both for a moment. The sun has almost completely set, and we simply enjoy the view, waiting for the colors to fade and darkness to settle in before we talk about the darkness we both share.

When the last of the light leaves the sky, Langston finally talks.

"One year."

My head whips to him.

"You will stay on the island for one year. That's the timeline I'm giving you. One year to tell the truth. One year until you die."

My mouth dries. Now I wish I hadn't downed the scotch so quickly.

Langston notices, or it's a strange coincidence, because he picks up my glass and pours me more scotch. He then takes my hand and places the glass in it.

"Thanks," I whisper, my throat burning from the single word. I take a small sip, savoring it this time.

"Every night I will give you the opportunity to extend your time or reduce it. If you lie, your time shrinks, and I will punish you. If you tell the truth, you gain time, and your time here will be more enjoyable."

One year.

I'm still caught on that part.

I can't stay on this island for a whole year.

Langston said I would die in one year. Death doesn't scare me, but the thought of being trapped this long, even in this beautiful of a place, sends icy blades jolting down my spine.

"During the day, you can spend your time however you want. Check out the island, swim, read a book, plan your escape, I don't care. But you will spend it away from me."

My eyes narrow, and my forehead wrinkles. "Why?"

"Why do you think?" he breathes, his breath full of warm

alcohol. He's had more than the single scotch to drink tonight.

I don't answer. I honestly don't know why he hates me so much.

"At night, you can sleep in my bed or be locked up."

"Locked up. There is no way I'd be able to sleep with you in my bed," I retort without a thought.

His fist tightens around his glass, but he doesn't say anything.

"This is where you'll meet me every night after the sun sets. You'll make your choice—tell me a truth to gain more time alive, or lie and lose time. Depending on what you tell me, I'll decide how much time to add or take away. Or…" He stops and takes another swig of his scotch.

"Or you tell me every truth on your half of that piece of paper right now and I'll let you live."

I purposefully don't look at him as he speaks. Langston is a good liar when he wants to be. His sparkling ocean eyes, his bright smile, his sun-kissed hair all make him look like a handsome lifeguard about to save me.

But he's like medusa, one look at him and he's deadly. His look can kill.

I know his tricks, though, so I don't look. I don't listen to the timbre of his voice or the shift of his weight in the sand. I definitely don't listen to my own heart, because that sucker just wants to get laid.

No, I take my cues from the wind, the ocean, the stars. I listen to the truth that only the world holds. There is no listening to Langston.

He knows there is no way I'm telling him what's on my half of the letter, a letter he ripped and stole. A letter he should have never even known about.

"What did I do to deserve death?" I continue to look at the ocean instead of him.

Our relationship is complicated; it always has been. We've saved each other as much as we've tormented each other. Protected each other as often as we've thrown the other to the wolves. And yet, we've never threatened to kill each other.

I'm missing something—something vital.

"You know what you've done. You may not realize that I know, but I do. Just think about the worst thing you've ever done and start there. That's why you deserve to die."

He pauses.

"I'm giving you a way out. You can live if you tell me everything tonight—right here, right now. This is your only chance to tell the full truth. Tell me the truth tonight, and I'll save you. Tell me a lie, and you've sealed your fate. This is a one time offer. Take it or leave it. Life or death."

I chuckle. "God, you are such an impatient man." Finally, I look at him and take in his big frustrated eyes, his ruffled blonde hair, and his stern lips. I'm used to smiling Langston. As a kid, he would always rather be playing than stewing in his anger.

"Impatient or not, I'd take my offer. Save yourself."

"You mean, tell you the truth so you will have no use for me and will kill me faster?"

He growls.

I growl back, but it's the truth. No matter what I choose, I'll end up dead at Langston's hand if I don't figure out a way to stop him. The only way I live is to be more valuable to him alive than dead. As long as I have my secrets, I'll stay alive.

But I'll be trapped.

"What will it be, Liesel?"

I fold my knees up and rest my arm against my knee, holding my glass. I stare at it, wishing we could both just tell the truth.

I'm not afraid of death—I just don't want to die at Langston's hands.

I spot the tattoo I got on the inside of my wrist.

I smile, knowing the story I'm going to tell tonight.

———

It's been one month since I was raped.

My life is spiraling.

And no one has noticed.

One. Whole. Month.

I walk into high school on the first day of my senior year expecting everyone to notice that I'm different, that everything has changed.

My locker is next to Enzo's.

I walk up to my shiny red locker where Enzo, Langston, and Zeke are gathered.

"Really? You couldn't let his best friends have the locker right next to him? Now, we have to deal with your overpowered perfume smell, glitter, and bobby pins every time we want to come to our lockers," Zeke complains like a bitch.

"Trust me, I'd rather not be stuck between Enzo and Zeke —the Sasquatch. Now I'll have to deal with your sweaty odor, hair ties, and hair that escapes your stupid man bun."

Langston snickers at my zing.

Enzo smiles.

Zeke looks ready to kill.

And I've never welcomed that look from Zeke more.

If no one is going to save me, the least they could do is kill me.

"What class you got first period, Liesel?" Enzo asks.

"Calculus."

Langston starts rolling in laughter.

"What's so funny?" I ask, thinking I have something stuck in my ponytail. I hardly bothered to get dressed for school today. The boys should notice that I'm not wearing my usual skintight dress, heels, curls, and makeup. Instead, I'm wearing ripped jeans, flats, a plain black v-neck, and my hair in a ponytail. I look like most girls around me, except, I'm not most girls.

I'm Liesel Dunn—glamorous, spirited, take no prisoners with my curvy hips and sassy words. I rule this school with my good looks even though I have exactly five dresses—one for each day of the week that I scrapped to save enough money to buy. No one cares that you don't have money when you walk with confidence like I do.

"There is no way you are going to pass calculus; you can barely do basic addition."

I flip him off, which makes the immature asshole laugh even more.

I have no hope that Langston or Zeke will notice, but Enzo should.

Unfortunately, he hasn't noticed me hiding out all summer.

He hasn't noticed that I haven't swum in the pool since that day. Or that I haven't worn anything except bags for clothes to cover my body.

I haven't hung out with Enzo or the guys for weeks.

I haven't asked for a second kiss.

I haven't asked for more.

Instead, I'm hiding and trying to move on.

"Nah, Liesel is smarter than you two idiots," Enzo says, defending me to his friends.

I smile—it's fake, but when Enzo smiles back at me, it turns genuine. Butterflies swarm in my belly as the familiar aches of being around Enzo return. After everything that happened, I still want him. His father didn't take those feelings away.

He took more.

"Enzo! Walk me to class?" Bridget says, pushing her way into the group and grabbing Enzo's hand.

My smile vanishes, gone from my face in one swipe.

Langston and Zeke give each other mischievous smirks.

Enzo throws his arm around her shoulder and walks her to class with Langston and Zeke strutting behind them.

They ignore me.

They forget about me.

They don't see my pain.

I'm nobody to them.

I never make it to class.

Instead, I walk out of the building.

I walk to the beach.

And then I sit on the sand watching the world go by. I watch the sun rise high in the sky. I watch it fall below the edge of the water.

I'm alone. I have no one.

I pick up my glass water bottle and slam it on the ground, wishing I had something stronger than water.

Soon, I won't need anything.

The glass breaks into several pieces.

I pick up one of the pieces under the darkness of night. The piece has a sharp edge—it will do.

Looking up at the sky with tears in my eyes, I slice through my wrist until it's deep enough to hit a vein.

The second I do, a calmness passes through me.

I've taken back control. My life is mine again. This is where it ends.

Pain creeps through my veins slowly, but I feel it. I feel all of it.

It makes me cry—not from the pain, but from the existing. From feeling something when I haven't felt anything in weeks.

I can still feel.

One last time.

My head starts spinning. I feel weak and tired, so tired.

I fall back onto the sand.

Finally, I managed to kill someone—me.

———

I look up at Langston sitting on the sand, listening to my story.

That was the last time I remember crying.

The last time tears fell down my face.

I hold out my wrist where the scar remains but is now covered with a tattoo of the word 'beautifully.'

"I killed myself that day."

Langston shakes his head. "No, you survived."

"No, the girl I was before that day flowed out from my veins. I killed her. I used to be kind, sweet, forgiving. After that, I became cynical, angry, bitchy. I became evil."

Langston narrows his eyes, not sure what I'm going to say next or why I'm telling this story.

"How did you survive?" Langston asks with a heavy breath.

I stare at him, unblinking.

We both know the truth, but I won't give him any credit.

"The devil saved me. He thought he was doing me a favor. He didn't know he was only saving a monster."

He looks away from me back out at the ocean. "Then, you got the tattoo so you wouldn't have to walk around with the reminder every day."

I look back at my wrist. "No, I got the tattoo to remind myself that I died beautifully, and that the beauty within me is now gone. All that remains is the wicked."

"At least that's the truth," he mutters under his breath.

Our eyes meet again, cutting through each other.

We both know who found me that night.

I still don't know why Langston saved me. I don't know how he found me. I don't know what happened. I just woke up in his arms.

"You won't kill me, Langston. I'll kill myself before you ever get the chance."

20

LANGSTON

THE TRUTH IS GOING to kill me.

I realize that after listening to Liesel's second story. I didn't think she'd get this deep with her stories this quickly, but she dove in head first. She flirted so closely with telling the complete truth, but twisted one tiny detail to make the story dig in like a knife to my heart.

It wasn't so much a lie as an omission.

She didn't include me in her story.

I noticed her when she showed up at school. I had been waiting for weeks to get to see her in one of her slinky school dresses.

My mouth almost fell open when I saw her in jeans. She still looked hotter than sin, and her muscled legs looked fantastic in her skinny jeans, but I knew something was wrong.

I thought she was pissed at Enzo.

I thought they were together.

I thought he had moved on and dumped her for Bridgett like I knew he would.

Then Liesel disappeared.

She didn't show up in any of our classes.

She didn't come to her locker.

She didn't sit with us at lunch.

She was gone.

I had to find her, clearly something terrible had happened.

I ran back to the club where I worked for Enzo's father. I pulled up all the security cameras I could find. But I didn't find her at the house, the club, or any of the properties Enzo's family owns.

She wasn't at the guest house or the house she grew up in either.

She was gone.

There was only one place she could have gone—the ocean.

It took me all day to find her.

When I did, she was passed out. Blood spilled from her wrist onto the sand.

I had killed before but never saved.

Until then.

That night I saved her.

"I regret it," I say.

"What?"

"I. Regret. It."

We stare into each other's eyes, and we both know what I'm talking about without saying it—I regret saving her. I wouldn't be in this mess if I had just let her die. If I hadn't searched for her that day. If I hadn't found her.

"Me too," she snaps back.

I nod.

She lets out a deep breath as she pulls her knees to her chest.

"I lied," Liesel says.

I let a beat go by before I answer her.

"I know."

Just like I know that she didn't want to die that day. She wanted the pain to end. She didn't want to be alone.

Liesel opens her mouth to speak, but I beat her to it.

"Come on—bedtime," I say.

I snatch her glass and put it back in the bag along with mine. Then, I pick up the towel we were sitting on and pack it in the bag before I start walking toward the house.

Liesel keeps step with me, walking by my side instead of behind me, almost like we shared a connection, instead of more lies.

I drop the bag off in the kitchen, and then head up the stairs.

Liesel follows silently, but I can feel the apprehension flowing off her.

We reach the top floor before I stop.

"Last chance, my bed or locked up?"

"Locked up," she says fiercely.

It pisses me off.

I may not be able to handle her near me during the day, but at night, I want her with me. Her words feed the monster inside me.

An idea forms to persuade her.

"Follow me," I say.

Liesel does. She chooses her moments, and it seems she's going to fight me with her lies, not her fists.

I lead her into my bedroom.

She stops abruptly in the doorway. "I said I wouldn't sleep in your bed."

"I'm not asking you to sleep in my bed." I walk over to the closet door and open it.

"This is the only room in the house that doesn't have a window or door for you to climb out of."

She smirks. "Why did you let me roam around the beach when you knew I escaped?"

"Because I don't care how you spend your days. I just care about your nights."

She tugs on her robe, closing it tighter around her waist.

She hasn't asked for clothes.

And if I know her, her stubborn ass won't.

She can pull it as tightly around her as possible, but it can't hide her body from me. The robe is too big for her, which somehow makes it easier to see the swell of her breasts and the muscles of her legs. The rest of her, though, is left up to my imagination, at least for tonight.

"Don't test my patience, Liesel. Get in the closet or get in my bed."

I won't chase her if she runs; I won't have to. She wants to act strong and tough, as if I don't affect her. Her body tells the real story though—the storm brewing in her eyes, the way she's biting her plump lip, the way she's twisting her body away.

Her eyes run down my body, and she notices that my cock is straining in my pants for her.

Before I can say anything, she runs into the closet like that's going to save her.

I move to close the door.

"You lost a week of time for lying."

"What about my punishment?"

My jaw ticks. "Goodnight, Liesel."

Then I close the door, locking her in my dark closet.

I pull out my phone and text Joel.

Liesel is in my closet. Do your worst.

I grab my tennis shoes by my bedroom door and slip them on. I pull my shirt off and head out into the night for a run.

This time, I won't be here to save her.

LIESEL

Langston won't forget about my punishment.

The door closes shut with a hard thud, followed by a clink of the lock.

I grip the handle, feeling Langston still standing on the other side of the door. I press my other hand to the door, and I feel his hot desire.

Why didn't he rape me?

Why didn't he kiss me? Touch me? Force himself on me?

I know he'll punish me. He won't forget.

I made sure the lies I've told stung. I may not be able to escape, I may not be able to fight back physically, but I can inflict pain with my words.

I hear footsteps and then nothing.

He's gone.

It's still early. *Maybe he headed back downstairs for another drink before bed?* I wish I had drunk more, then maybe I'd be able to sleep in this dark closet.

He put me in a fucking closet—*the bastard.*

I feel around the walls, hoping for a big pile of clothes to sleep on. All I feel is drywall.

He removed all the fucking clothes!

My back hits the wall in the farthest corner of the dark closet before I slump down to the floor.

I can't see an inch in front of me in the darkness.

Langston left me alone in a pitch-black, box of a room. *Maybe my punishment is sleeping in the darkness with my nightmares?* He doesn't know that it's not the darkness or the nightmares that I'm afraid of.

The pain I feel comes from somewhere else—something Langston will never understand.

I squeeze my eyes shut, hoping the pain and torment won't come for me tonight. There are only two ways to keep the pain out: sleep and sex.

Sleep isn't going to happen for hours. I'm used to living on very little sleep. And there is no way I'll be able to fall asleep on this cold, hard floor.

I can do something about the other option.

The one good thing about being locked in a dark closet is that there are no cameras in here.

When I fucked Waylon all night, I did it as much for the cameras, for Langston, as I did it for me. I put on a show for Langston, showed him what he can never have.

Tonight is all about me. I need this. I need the distraction. Langston doesn't get to watch me pleasure myself.

I grab the strap of the robe, untie it, and let the robe fall open.

Instinctively, I look up into the corner to double-check there isn't a camera. If there is one, I can't see it. And if Langston is watching, an uneasy feeling will take hold of me.

None does.

There is no camera.

I purse my lips as I let out a breath, trying to relax. This is my happy place—fucking.

I can't fuck Waylon, but I can fuck myself.

I close my eyes, tuning out the world.

It helps that the room is silent. I can't hear Langston.

So why do I keep thinking about him?

He's holding me captive and has threatened to kill me —that's why.

Stop thinking about Langston!

I open my eyes, staring out at the darkness.

Focus.

I bring my knees toward me, placing my feet flat on the floor and letting my legs fall apart, wide and open.

My hands take their time exploring my own body. It's been a long time since I've needed to get myself off. Waylon keeps me more than satisfied.

And before that, it was Jason, Andrew, Carter...

The men in my life have been endless.

My hands start sensually exploring with a light touch down my neck. My skin is soft and hot beneath my fingers. My breasts feel large in my hands. Down I trail my hand over the softness of my stomach, purposefully avoiding any scars that remind me of my old life, before I feel between my legs.

I'm dry, not wet.

I haven't done nearly enough to turn myself on yet.

My hand rises back up, and I suck slowly on my fingers, providing moisture to turn myself on.

I use one hand to spread my pussy lips and the other to find my clit. I rub my saliva over my clit, warming myself up. I move slowly; I have all night after all. There is no pressure to come quickly.

It's been so long since I've touched myself like this that I've forgotten what I like—*slow, light pressure or fast, hard pressure. Do I like a circular motion or the flick of my fingers over my sensitive bud?*

Soon, I find my rhythm. I'm breathy, warm, and my heartbeat is pounding.

That's when I slip a finger inside.

I'm wet—but barely.

"Jesus Christ."

I think of Waylon—of his tanned skin, his thick rippling muscles, his perfectly plump cock.

I pump two fingers in and out, concentrating on Waylon.

I get minimally wetter.

Dammit.

I remove my fingers in frustration.

I know what will turn me on—a stubborn asshole who locked me in a closet but not before giving me a panty-melting, hungry glare. One that tore through my robe and told me he knows exactly what to do with my body.

With Waylon, I had to teach him how to turn me on. I have a feeling Langston would just know. There would be no need for instructions. He'd sense what I needed; understand me more than I do myself.

I won't let my mind think about Langston.

I can make myself come without a man's help.

My fingers return to my pussy as I focus on my breathing. I pump in and out of myself while my thumb circles my swollen clit.

A low moan hums through my belly, bringing me closer to the beautiful explosion my body is capable of making.

Footsteps creep outside the floor, startling me.

"Fuck," I curse under my breath.

I was so close to coming.

Who am I kidding? I wasn't anywhere close.

I remove my fingers and fumble with the robe, tying it around my waist.

I'm sure it's just Langston returning to go to sleep, but the heaviness of the footsteps concern me. Langston can move silently if he wants. All of Enzo's men can. Enzo taught them how to move like ninjas before they turned ten.

The fact that I can hear the creak of each step tells me he wants me to hear him.

Maybe he saw what I was doing and thought he'd interrupt? Make me sexually frustrated all night? Maybe that's my punishment?

The footsteps stop.

I hold my breath, listening carefully for Langston in the bathroom or climbing into bed.

Will it be easier or harder to touch myself knowing he's so near?

I guess I'm about to find out.

Clank.

I hear scratching at the door. The sound of the lock turns, followed by the door. A sliver of moonlight creeps in behind him, illuminating his outline, but hiding his face.

"Langston?" I breathe out. He's returned to punish me, I have no doubt.

He doesn't answer me. He walks silently toward me, his feet sounding loud and heavy.

He's trying to scare me, prepare me, for what he's about to do to me.

But I'm one step ahead of him.

He squats down in front of me and takes my hand in his.

"You smell that?" I ask, my voice is raspy.

He lifts my fingers to his face and takes a deep inhale. There is no mistaking what my fingers smell like: sex.

He growls low and deep. The sound vibrates through my body—the missing piece to my arousal.

He grips me hard on the biceps, pinning me against the wall with his legs between my knees and thighs.

I don't know what he has planned as punishment for me, and I don't care.

Right now, I need to come. I need to chase the demons inside my head away.

I grab Langston's hand and tear it from my bicep. He

thinks I'm going to fight him, that I can't handle his touch. Just the opposite. My body is begging for a man's touch.

I spread my legs wider. And although I can't see Langston's face, I know he's shocked.

His heart rate is about to double in speed.

Carefully, I pull his fingers to my mouth and suck viciously. I let my teeth scrape harder than I should, but I want his fingers nice and wet before he touches me. Then, I glide his fingers to my entrance.

"Fuck me," I whisper.

His fingers don't move from my slit, but they don't push inside me either.

I'm impatient and needy. I won't wait.

I grab his hand and push his fingers inside me.

I gasp as I grip onto his shirt with one hand, and keep my other around his wrist.

"Fuck me, Langston."

I guide his hand in and out. Eventually, he starts moving his fingers in and out on his own accord.

My head falls back against the wall, and I spread open wider for him so he can get deeper inside me.

Langston takes full advantage.

"Yes," I moan as he pounds his fingers inside me.

I bite my lip, and he pushes again and again.

"More," I breathe. "I need more."

It takes him a moment to catch my meaning, but he pushes a second, then a third finger, inside.

"Oh, god, yes!" I moan, no longer forming coherent thoughts in my head.

It feels incredible, but he has yet to touch my clit. Probably because he thinks if he doesn't touch me there, then I won't gain pleasure. Then this is still a form of punishment.

Ha.

There is nothing punishing about this.

I grab his other hand and slide his fingers over my clit.

"Rub," I order.

He growls again but complies.

He starts rubbing, but his fingers only manage a couple of rubs before he slips off my clit.

Damn, Langston!

There is a loud sound.

Langston stills.

"I'm so close," I exhale.

He ignores me.

Then, suddenly, his fingers are gone.

And then, so is he.

No!

He doesn't get to get me all worked up and then not finish me.

I jump off the ground and run to the door.

It's open.

I run out and chase Langston down the hallway. I don't care if an army is attacking us, he better come finish what he started right now.

I don't make it far until I run into a brick wall of a chest.

I stop abruptly.

His fingers hold me back at the waist.

A light flickers on.

Langston's angry glare leaves me timid and weak at the knees.

His eyes roam up and down my body, like he's taking inventory of it.

A soft breeze blows through the window. It's then I realize I'm naked. My robe must have fallen off as I was chasing after him.

His eyes heat on the scar on my stomach.

I move my hands to cover it, but he gently and firmly removes my hand so he can inspect my scar.

"Are you ready to sleep in my bed?" he asks sternly.

"No."

"Then what are you doing out of the closet?"

"I—I, uh, just wanted to know why you stopped. What you were chasing?"

"Go back to bed, Liesel."

"What about—"

"Now!" His booming voice demands compliance.

I have no choice but to walk back to the closet.

I find my robe on the floor and cover my body. Once again, I find myself slumping in the corner of the closet.

He walks to the door, and this time, I see his eyes before he closes the door. They brand into me, hiding his thoughts but making it clear he's angry with me.

Then the door is shut and locked.

I'm left alone once again.

Once again with my demons.

Once again to finish myself.

I huff, knowing there is no way I'm going to come now. Tonight, I'm going to have to deal with my monsters.

To make things worse, I've shown Langston how weak I am for his body. Now he has an even bigger advantage. I need to figure out how to get the upper hand. I need to get ahold of a phone and call Waylon, Siren, or Kai. Anyone who might search and find me.

Or I could strike my own deal with Langston. One that keeps him from touching me during the day, but at night…

22

LANGSTON

I WAKE BEFORE THE SUN—NOT that I slept. I couldn't after what happened with Liesel last night.

The woman is the most irritating, confounding, frustrating woman on the planet. She's also the most intriguing, alluring, beautiful woman.

And that means I'm fucked.

I should stay away, except when I'm pushing her to spill her secrets, but I can't. I want to fuck her so badly. My balls are blue just thinking about it.

I can't.

I can do many things to Liesel—torture her, demand truths, even kill her. I just can't fuck her.

Dammit, do my balls ache. My cock is stiff as a board, and after thirty minutes of trying to jack myself off, I'm more sexually frustrated than I was when I started. Finally, I just give up and decide to start my day.

I flick the lock on the door and wait, but Liesel doesn't move inside the closet.

I listen carefully and hear her soft snoring—she's asleep.

She'll figure out soon enough that the door is unlocked.

175

I head downstairs and find Amelia in the kitchen.

"Oh, Langston, I don't have coffee made yet. I wasn't expecting you to wake up for another hour like you usually do," Amelia says.

I grunt and make my way to the coffee machine. I don't usually operate it, but I'm too tired for words. I take the bag of coffee beans and put them into the hand grinder. I begin grinding when the handle pops off.

"Son of a bitch." I slam the grinder down on the counter—beans and broken metal fly everywhere.

I breathe heavily, realizing I need a release, any release. I need to get far away from the blonde upstairs.

"Let me work on your coffee for you," Amelia says, taking what remains of the grinder from my hands.

I nod and place my hands on my head as I storm out of the kitchen.

I should go for a run. Or meditate. Or swim. Something healthy to get my pent up frustration out.

Instead, I go see Joel.

I'm not sure if it will help or make things worse, but I need to see him. I need answers to what happened last night.

Joel is one of my trusted men who lives in the house with me, so I don't have to go far.

I walk to his door, letting my feet hit the floor roughly so he can hear me coming. When I knock, the sound is loud enough to wake the entire house up.

I can hear him moving in his bed, and then his feet hit the floor as he runs to answer the door. He knows it's me. He knows I have questions for him.

He opens the door without a shirt on. His hair is a disheveled mess, and a five o'clock shadow covers his face.

"Yes?" he asks as he grips the doorframe.

"What happened last night?"

He frowns. "Nothing. Nothing happened."

My eyes scan his face, looking for the truth.

For the first time, I wish I had cameras in my bedroom so I could know for sure if he's telling the truth.

"Did you do what I asked?"

Joel's eyes linger behind me, and I realize that Liesel has woken up. Probably my knocking or the blunder with the coffee grinder jolted her into the morning.

I glare at Joel.

I don't care that Liesel is standing behind us watching the exchange. I want to know what happened from his mouth because Lord knows I don't trust a word out of Liesel's.

"Yes," he answers before closing the door.

I turn and glance at Liesel but don't speak to her. She's still wearing that damn robe, even though she can't seem to keep it on her body all the time. She won't ask for clothes, but I won't survive her staying here a year without her completely covered in layers.

Liesel's eyes follow me while I walk back to the kitchen.

"Amelia, get Liesel some clothes and make sure she's wearing them by the time I get back."

Amelia blushes with a knowing smile as Liesel enters the kitchen.

"Langston, can we—" Liesel starts.

"I'm taking the helicopter to the other side of the island. Don't worry about lunch or dinner for me today, Amelia."

Liesel's mouth snaps shut. Finally, she understands I won't be talking to her during the day. My only use for her is at night.

I walk away from Liesel before she has a chance to open her sassy mouth.

I'm grumpy, annoyed, and sex-deprived. And based on how Liesel is telling her stories, I know what story she's going to tell next.

I'm terrified of her lying about the next part of her story.

I'm more terrified if she finally decides to tell the truth.

One of us might end up dead tonight.

Or worse—I'll lose control and fuck her. Although, from the way her body responded to me last night, she just might enjoy that.

————

I'm not surprised to find Liesel already sitting on the beach as the sun begins to set.

She's wearing a red bikini top and jean shorts. Her skin is more tanned than it was this morning. She must have spent the day in the sun.

Meanwhile, I spent the day in torment.

I readjust the bag on my shoulder as I walk down to the beach to meet her. I'm glad she's wearing clothes; I just wish she was wearing more clothes.

The waves crash against the shore as I take a seat next to her. I don't bother with a towel this time. We sit directly on the sand tonight.

Once again, I pull out two lowball glasses and pour them with Liesel's favorite scotch. Luckily, it's my favorite scotch too.

She takes her glass, and we drink, watching the waves and the setting sun.

Clouds are covering most of the sun. Instead of the vibrant yellows, oranges, and reds that usually paint the sky, tonight's sunset is muted. It's gray and pale yellow. It's fitting for the conversation we are about to have.

"Care to skip ahead to the part about what your half of the letter says? Or just skip the next couple of years of our past? Maybe tell a happy story. I'm in a foul mood."

She smirks. "Why? Didn't get good sleep last night?"

I lift my glass to my lips. *I'm going to need a lot of alcohol to get through tonight.* "Something like that."

"Try sleeping on the hard floor of a closet. Then you can complain."

"You are welcome in my bed anytime."

She bites her lip but doesn't take me up on my offer.

"That's what I thought." We both finish our drinks. I take the bottle and pour more scotch into our glasses.

"You're terrified of what I'm going to say, aren't you?"

I roll my shoulders back. "No."

"We can always tell when we are lying to each other. You're grumpy, sleep-deprived, and antsy. And you're a shot away from being drunk. You only get like this when I get under your skin."

"Start talking before I decide to take away a month of your life."

Her eyes narrow at me.

"I'm going to enjoy this," she says.

That makes one of us.

"I had three protectors. Three men who cared about me in very different ways. One claimed I drove him mad. That I was a spoiled little princess even though I didn't have a penny to my name. That I took more than I gave," she starts her story.

Zeke—she's talking about our friend Zeke who always found Liesel annoying. But he never took the time to get to know her like Enzo and I did.

"One claimed to love me. He stole kisses, fucked me senseless, gave me everything—money, clothes, college tuition."

Enzo. Her words burn through me like a raging fire. She's trying to get me irritated before she gets to the hard part. But it's all difficult. Hearing that she fucked him, even though I already knew it, hurts.

"And one claimed to be my best friend. He claimed to protect me, to kill for me. He couldn't offer me money, or love, or kindness, but he could offer me his protection."

Me—she's talking about me.

"All three failed. I could have forgiven them the first time. I did forgive them. I moved on with my life. I went back to school and started flirting with Enzo again. But when they failed twice, I was well beyond forgiveness."

I squeeze my eyes shut to block out the pain.

I should blame myself for how Liesel turned out. I failed her. Sure, Enzo and Zeke should have known as well. We all should have protected her. But this is my biggest failure, and she's about to rub it in my face.

I deserve every bit of pain I'm about to endure.

I should apologize for my failure.

I should beg for her forgiveness.

But I'll do neither.

I don't deserve compassion.

And there are no words to apologize for what I've done.

Liesel has stopped talking.

"Keep going. I deserve to know the pain I caused."

"Why? So you can get off on it?" her head whips to me.

"No, so I can do penance."

"Like you care at all. You're going to kill me! You don't care about my pain."

"Then do it for the boy who once did."

She blinks rapidly, looking at me.

"Enzo's father raped me a second time. I won't go into the gory details, but he would have raped me again and again…" her voice falters as she speaks.

"The first time, I was able to survive it. Somehow I went back to my normal life. After getting raped again, everything changed."

She finishes her glass.

I pick up the bottle to pour her more, but she shakes her head.

Uneasily, I put the bottle back down in the sand.

"Six weeks later, I found out I was pregnant."

Her words squeeze around my heart. I already knew she was pregnant, but it still hurts that she went through that alone.

"Did you tell anyone?" I ask, wondering if Enzo knew. Her mother, anyone? I clearly wasn't worthy of the news. She didn't think I would help her, protect her.

"No. The first person I told was a nurse at an abortion clinic."

There is so much agony in her voice. So much outrage at what she had to endure in solitude.

She was raped—twice.

And everyone in her life who was supposed to protect her failed.

I failed.

And then worst of all, none of us realized anything was wrong.

I saw something was different and still didn't protect her. I didn't hold her hand when she went to the clinic. I did nothing.

Liesel purses her lips and blows through them. She's trying not to cry.

Her and me both.

"What stopped you from going through with it?"

She bites her bottom lip, rolling it around between her teeth.

"The child's father did."

"Jesus," I curse. Enzo's father stopped her.

I didn't know that part of the story. It's bad enough the bastard raped her, but then he forced her to have his child.

She shakes her head. "He told me if I aborted our child, he'd just rape me again and again until I got pregnant.

"I never wanted to have children. Especially not as a teenager, but I had no choice," she says.

I should have been there. I should have helped her.

"After graduation, I ran. I told everyone I was taking a gap year before I went to college. Enzo had given me some money, and he'd already paid for my college. No one questioned why I wanted to take a break before school.

"I ran. I hid. And I had the baby—alone. Then I made the choice to give him up—alone. That was the hardest thing I've ever done," she whimpers.

Sharp pain shoots through my body at her words. I tracked her every day of her trip. I watched her from afar. I knew the truth, and I did nothing. I let her be by herself.

I pound my fists into the ground, trying to hold back the tears.

Liesel was my best friend growing up.

Until everything changed.

Until she started chasing Enzo instead of hanging with me.

Until I fucked it all up by not keeping my word.

Until I made a promise that ensured I would stay away from her forever.

I put my hand on the ground behind me as I lean back.

Somehow, my hand finds hers.

Our fingers intertwine.

We sit on the beach, holding hands like lovers.

"Did you know? Did you know that I was pregnant? That I was raped?"

I squeeze her hand as my tears finally fall.

She doesn't cry, though.

She never cries.

"No," I lie.

Her teeth grind together as she nods.

She's the strong one. She's the one who doesn't cry.

If things were different, if I had the power to forgive her, I probably would, but I don't have that power.

And what I did to her is just as unforgivable.

I let go of her hand and stand up, wading into the water until the waves crash against my feet.

Liesel was raped, had a baby, and let him go. And all I did was watch from the sidelines, thinking I was doing the right thing.

No, I did do the right thing, even though it killed me.

Liesel did one decent thing—give up her baby for adoption. Still, it doesn't forgive her for what she did after.

"I hate you, Liesel, but not because of this. You saving that baby, getting him away from Enzo's father, that was the bravest thing you've ever done. I hate myself for not being there for you."

"I hate you for not being there that night. But I hate you more for trapping me here and threatening to kill me. What did I do to make you hate me like this?"

I ignore her question. "Thank you for the truth. You gained back the week you lost yesterday."

Then I walk back into the house—a broken, weak man. I'm afraid of what I'm going to do next. Weak men only make mistakes.

2 3

LIESEL

LANGSTON THINKS I told the truth, maybe because he wants it to be the truth.

I hate children.

I wanted to be childless.

I was forced to have the baby.

I wanted to give my baby up.

I'm not sure which parts of the story are truths and which are lies. That's not true. I know, I just can't admit the truth. It's too painful.

But there is one big part that I lied about.

Giving my child up was the hardest thing I've ever done. It was torment. That was the last time I remember crying. The last time I remember feeling anything. After that, I became numb. I became a bitch a hundred percent of the time instead of most of the time.

It doesn't shock me to think that Langston thinks everything I said was the truth. He wants to believe what I said was as awful as it gets. That I have a child out there somewhere, and I gave him up rather than have his rapist father hunt and search for him.

185

After my child was adopted, I was shocked that Enzo's father never came to claim him. I thought he was just biding his time.

Thank God, he's dead now. I'd do it myself if he wasn't.

My heart bleeds on the inside. For once, I wish I could cry, could show real emotion. But if I ever started, I would never stop.

Langston cried, though.

He can still feel pain.

And I can still tell when he's lying.

Langston knew I was pregnant.

He knew I was raped.

He knew I was alone when I gave the baby up.

He was always watching me.

Langston could have been there with me.

He could have held my hand as I gave birth.

He could have wiped my tears when my baby was taken from my arms.

I hate him.

Whatever I did to make him hate me now was warranted. He left me all alone. He made me like this.

Langston starts the climb up the cliffside back to the house.

He stirred emotions deep inside me, forcing me to re-evaluate my needs. Usually, I just fight with my words. And my words hurt Langston. But I want more than his tears; I want his blood.

I run at Langston.

I know he hears me, but he doesn't stop me.

He lets me tackle him hard into the side of the cliff. I jump on his back as my fists pound into his head over and over, hoping to bludgeon him to death.

Only after I've gotten a few good punches in does he grab my wrist to stop me and twist me around to his front. I wrap my legs around his waist and continue beating his chest with my free hand.

"You're a fucking liar! You knew! You fucking knew!"

I hit him so hard that he falls back onto the sand with me straddling him. I hit his chest over and over.

My frustration is building, brick by brick, as I pummel him repeatedly.

He lets me.

He lets me hurt him.

I need a release.

I try so hard to cry, to let out the emotions I'm keeping inside, but none come.

I scream—it's a high pitched, glass shattering kind of scream. But it's not a release, not a real display of emotions.

Finally, Langston grabs my wrists, forcing me to stop.

"I'm going to kill you. You say that I can't kill, but that's only because I've been saving my first kill for you."

"Are you finished?"

"No, you fucking liar."

"Yes, I lied."

My breath catches. *I can't believe he admitted that.*

"I knew you were raped. I knew you were pregnant. I knew you gave the baby up."

Heart. Beating. So. Fast.

"You knew?" My voice is soft, still not fully believing it until this moment.

He nods. "I knew."

"Why didn't you tell me? Why didn't you approach me? Help me?"

He shakes his head. "Sorry, huntress. You can know that I lied, but you don't get to know the rest."

I hit him as hard as I can muster in his chest.

"I can't believe you. I—I don't understand how you are

mad at me. Why do you want to kill me? You were the one who knew and did nothing. You betrayed me!"

"Think really hard. Your only chance at redemption is to tell me what's on your half of the letter. And even that won't earn my forgiveness. I won't be merciful."

"Then we will both die hating each other," I vow.

My entire body is pain. I need a release. I need to forget.

Langston notices.

"Can't cry, can you?"

I shake my head slowly.

He smirks. "And you haven't orgasmed since you came here either?"

I shake my head and look away.

He turns my head back until I'm looking at him.

"At least when I die, I'll die after coming."

"Fuck you."

"You wish."

I growl.

"Now, which will it be? My bed or the closet?"

I roll off of him and stomp all the way to the fucking closet.

———

I roll over on the hard, cool ground in the closet.

Then I turn the other way.

Back and forth. Tossing and turning.

The floor is uncomfortable, and I don't have a blanket, but that's not why I can't sleep.

I stand up and begin pacing back and forth. I take five steps in one direction, then turn around and return my five steps.

It's pitch-black, but you would think my eyes would have adjusted to the darkness by now. They haven't. I still can't see, and if I miscount or take an extra-large step, I bump into the wall.

The pacing won't help me sleep, but I hope it will address my flooding urges. I feel my control slipping.

I rub the back of my neck—it's soaked in sweat, along with my forehead and neck. I'm sweating everywhere.

I'm hot, burning hot.

I need a release, but I don't know how to get one without a man.

Jesus, I'm fucked up.

If I could just cry, feel something, maybe I wouldn't feel this way. I don't know how to cry anymore.

And I don't know how to come alone.

I need help.

I storm to the door and grab the handle, knowing it's time I talked to Langston. I won't survive the year like this. If Langston wants a chance to get answers, then he needs to help me live long enough to be able to tell him the truth.

I rattle the doorknob, but it doesn't open.

"Fuck!"

I slam my hand on the door, pounding on it.

"Langston!"

Knock.

Knock.

Knock.

"Open the door! We need to talk!"

I press my ear up against the door, but I don't hear anything. If Langston is in his bed, he would have heard me. He's either ignoring me or not here.

He's never here for me when I need him.

My nails dig into the back of the door and then scrape down. I hope I'm destroying the perfect finish on this pretty door, but I doubt I am.

I collapse to my knees as I cry out, begging my body to surrender, to give in.

Cry, dammit.

Shed one fucking tear.

Make this easier.

I feel under my eyes, but all I sense is the sticky sweat clinging to my cheeks.

I'm broken.

As much as I don't want to admit it, I need Langston.

"Liesel?"

Langston's voice.

I exhale sharply.

"Yes," I croak back.

"What's wrong?"

Do it. Say it and get it over with.

"I need you."

There's a pause.

He's not going to answer. He's not going to talk to me. He's not going to help me.

The door opens.

No light shines in—the room remains dark as he steps inside the closet and then shuts the door behind him.

"I never got my reward for telling you the truth," I say.

I hear him swallow, but he still doesn't speak.

I stand up and shimmy my jean shorts down until they are a heap on the floor. He must have heard the flop my jeans made, but he doesn't react. At least, he doesn't react in a way I can see.

I reach up and untie my swimsuit top and let it fall to the floor. Lastly, I shove my bikini bottoms to the floor.

"I need a release, Langton. Fuck me. Make me come. I need it if you want me to survive long enough to spill my secrets."

He doesn't move.

I hate how desperate I am. I hate that I'll be cheating on Waylon, but I literally won't make it without this.

"I'm sorry, Waylon. Please forgive me."

I grab for Langston.

He doesn't move as I grip onto his bare chest. *He sleeps shirtless, does he sleep naked?*

My claws dig into his chest, sliding down his muscles until I find out.

He's wearing boxer briefs.

So sexy.

I can't see him, but I imagine him in my head.

No.

I don't need to imagine Langston. I just need his body.

"Sit down," I say, pushing his shoulders down.

I'm not sure if he will obey me. I'm not sure if he will take control and rape me.

As long as I'm in control of this, then it's my decision. Unfortunately, Langston has never been very good at letting me have control.

Surprisingly, he sits on the floor.

"Don't kiss me," I say, as I climb on top of him.

I find his cock hard as stone, lift it out of his shorts and let it push at my entrance.

I'm frustrated, worked up and horny as hell. I'm not sure if I'm wet, if I'm ready for him, but I'm too impatient to wait.

I slide down hard on top of his cock, my fingers digging into his shoulders as he tears through me. I wasn't wet enough, but I don't care.

I feel the pain.

I feel—that's enough.

"Now, I'm going to fuck you until you make me come."

I slide up and down his cock—hard and furiously fast.

I don't feel myself getting wetter, just hotter.

I thought fucking Langston would be explosive. I thought he'd know how to work my body, make me come in seconds.

He does, but I'm not letting him have control. That's why I'm not coming yet.

If I gave up control to him, then he'd have me panting and screaming his name in minutes.

I'm not going to give Langston control yet. That's one step too far. I need to come, but I need to control myself.

"Fuck," I moan as I ride him harder, rubbing my clit up against the deep V of his sculpted abs.

Faster.

Faster.

Faster.

Maybe if I kiss him? Just once?

Nope. That's too far.

I won't betray Waylon like that.

This isn't about cheating. It's about taking what I need to survive.

I rub myself against him, creating more friction.

I'm so hot, soaked in sweat, this is the moment…

"Liesel?" Langston's voice is so soft, full of pain and sadness. He knows I can't come. This won't work.

"I hate you. I hate you. I hate you. I hate you!" I pump over him, begging my body to give in.

I try one more time, but it doesn't happen.

I don't come.

It was all for nothing.

I shove him hard, and I climb off him.

I scream.

I pound my fists into the walls and consider pounding them into his head.

Before I can decide what to punch next, I collapse from exhaustion.

2 4

LANGSTON

WHAT THE HELL happened last night?

I yawn.

I'm going to need an IV of coffee to keep me going today. I didn't sleep more than five minutes all last night, not after what Liesel did.

How do I deal with her?

What the hell do I do?

Coffee. Coffee first, then I deal with Liesel.

I get dressed, flip the lock of the closet door, and race down the stairs. I know she didn't sleep a second last night, either. She'll be chasing me down the stairs, wanting answers.

I'm on a mission.

Coffee.

Liesel won't get in my way.

The damn grinder won't get in my way.

Not today.

I march down the stairs and over to the kitchen.

"Morning, boss," Amelia says with an annoying smile as she holds out a cup of coffee for me.

"Thanks," I grumble, grabbing the cup of coffee from her hands.

She smirks. "I figured you'd be up early again and need this."

"You're a lifesaver." I guzzle down the first cup and then help myself to a second.

"Didn't get much sleep last night?" She blushes, tossing her auburn hair over her shoulder. Amelia is a fantastic cook, but she's equally as capable equipped with a gun in her hand as she is a chef's knife.

"Don't ask."

I carry my cup of coffee outside onto the patio just as Liesel comes downstairs in her jean shorts and red bikini top again.

Jesus.

She's going to kill me.

And she's going to succeed long before I can kill her.

Less than a minute later, Liesel is opening the glass door and walking toward me carrying her own cup of coffee.

I frown.

I need to tell Amelia that the first pot of coffee in the morning is mine and to not share it with Liesel.

Liesel, unlike me, looks ready to go. Her blonde hair hangs in waves over her right shoulder. Her face looks bright with just a hint of freckles over her nose instead of the painted face I'm used to seeing on her. She looks young and carefree in her red bikini top that I want to rip from her body.

"I know you won't talk to me until the sun sets, but you should make an exception today," Liesel puts one hand on her hip while the other lifts her oversized mug to her lips, as she stands in front of me.

I shake my head and then press my fingers against my

forehead, trying to relieve the pressure from my pounding headache.

"You know what would fix your migraine? Talking to me," Liesel says.

Ignore her.

I keep my eyes closed, hoping she'll go away if I don't give her any attention.

"Really? You think ignoring me is going to work? We aren't kids anymore, Langston! This isn't a game. You can't just ignore me. You can't just do what you did last night and not talk to me."

Fuck.

I run my hand through my hair.

I don't want to talk about last night.

I don't want to think about last night.

Last night was one giant mistake.

Liesel steps closer to me, and I finally look at her.

She's right.

I should talk to her.

A buzz in my pocket brings me out from under her spell. I pull out my cell phone.

"Yes?" I answer without looking at who's calling me. I'm just thankful that someone is before I made another mistake.

"Siren's missing," Zeke says.

My heart stops. "What do you mean she's missing?"

Zeke has been my best friend for years. Siren, his wife, has a connection to my soul.

"I mean she was supposed to pick up Cayden from daycare, and she never showed up. I think someone kidnapped her."

Rage consumes me, and I welcome it. As much as I hate to admit it, I'd rather be dealing with Zeke's crisis than my own.

"I'll be there soon. We'll find her."

"Hurry," Zeke says.

I hang up and start marching inside, my shoulder brushes Liesel's as I pass, but I can't think about anything except getting back to Miami and finding Siren.

"Langston!" Liesel yells, following me inside.

I keep walking. *Ren, I'm coming.*

"Langston Pearce! Talk to me right now!"

I stop. I turn and look at her. "I don't have time for you to throw a tantrum right now, Liesel."

"I'm not throwing a tantrum. Just talk to me."

"Fine. Someone I love is in danger. And as you've pointed out, I have a habit of not being there for people when they need it. I'm not going to let her down."

Liesel's shoulders drop. Her lips curve into an O. Her breathing slows.

"Joel!" I yell.

He pops his head out of his room.

"You're on security, Joel. Make sure everyone is safe."

He nods.

"Amelia, you're in charge of the house."

She salutes me. "Yes, Captain."

I shake my head. Usually, I like her teasing. Not right now.

Amelia steps back, noticing my change in mood.

I jog over to the locked part of the house. I unlock and open the dividing door. "Phoenix," I holler.

She steps forward out of her bedroom, still wearing a robe.

"Yes?"

I glance back to Liesel.

"Phoenix, you're in charge of Liesel."

Liesel's eyebrows draw up.

I glance to Phoenix, and she nods solemnly.

Then I lock the door again and pull my phone out. I start

making calls to arrange for a flight, walking around the house with Liesel on my heels.

"How are you going to fly somewhere when you killed the pilot?" Liesel hollers.

"You killed Ken?" Joel asks.

I growl at him.

Joel moves out of my way and doesn't ask any other dumb questions.

Liesel, on the other hand, continues to run after me as I head to my car.

I unlock my Range Rover and open the door.

Liesel is there to grab the door before I climb inside.

"You didn't kill the pilot, did you?"

I don't answer her.

"You're a piece of work. You just did that to scare me."

She takes a step back.

"When will you be back?" she asks.

"When I save my girl."

My words cut her. She doesn't know who I'm talking about. All she hears is the *my girl* part. I'm talking about a woman I seem to care about more than her. I see the jealousy in her eyes.

When I return, Liesel will make me pay for that.

But just as quickly as it came, the jealousy is gone.

She wasn't able to do that before. I'm guessing it has to do with her having trouble feeling anything anymore.

"Whoever *she* is, save her like you didn't save me."

"I won't fail." I slam the door and drive away, while Liesel watches me leave her, like so many times before.

2 5

LIESEL

Who is the woman Langston dropped everything for? At a moment's notice no less, scrapping all of his plans for the day.

She's a lucky woman, whoever she is. Even when we were best friends, Langston never looked at me with that much worry or concern in his eyes. He never ran the second I called.

Who is she?

Who is he running to save?

Who does he love?

All those questions burn through my head as I watch Langston drive off.

Is she a girlfriend?

A woman he wishes was his?

Is it Kai or Siren?

Who?

It's like a punch to the gut. My world spins. My eyes slant into slits of anger.

199

I'm jealous.

For a split second, I wish I was the lucky girl to whom Langston is running.

"Snap out of it. Langston is a cruel, sadistic killer. Nobody wants to be loved by a man like that," I coach myself.

I walk back inside the house just as Joel heads back into his bedroom and slams the door shut. He doesn't care about protecting us. He's useless. I doubt I see him out of his room again.

I head into the kitchen, where Amelia is making breakfast. She's holding a plate of food, which I assume is for me.

"Thanks, I'll just eat it out—"

Amelia takes a bite of the toast on the plate. "There are groceries in the fridge. I hope you know how to cook."

She flashes me an annoying, sarcastic grin before she takes her breakfast out on the patio, where I usually eat it.

"Bitch," I mutter under my breath.

I'm alone.

And I'm not hungry.

I stare at the door Langston had to unlock to relay an instruction. There is a woman who lives in the other half of the house.

Who is she?

I walk to the solid wood door. I put my hand on the door handle and twist.

It's locked.

I jiggle the door handle a couple more times just to be sure, but the door is definitely locked.

I consider spending all my time trying to break in, but I have more important things to do today. I need to find a way off this island before Langston returns.

I run upstairs to Langston's bedroom.

I search for his phone, his laptop, any electronic device that I can use to contact Waylon.

God, Waylon, I miss him.

Langston is a bit of a minimalist. He has a nightstand with no drawers. His dresser only has clothes in the top two drawers and the bottom drawers are empty. His bathroom only holds the absolute basics—toothbrush, soap, towels. I find nothing useful.

I search all the guest bedrooms.

I search the library.

I search the kitchen, the dining room, the living room. I search the entire house but find no phone, no computer, no tablet. Nothing that can help me contact Waylon.

I grab a banana from the counter for energy, not bothering to cook anything while I think about what to do next.

My eyes linger on the door again.

The door that has remained locked the entire time I've been here.

It has to be locked for a reason.

My guess is a computer and phone sit on the other side of that door, maybe in Langston's office.

I shove the last bite of banana in my mouth while I listen carefully, trying to determine if anyone else is in the house.

I don't hear Amelia or Joel. I don't hear maids cleaning. The house is eerily quiet.

I grin and pull a bobby pin from my hair while I walk to the locked door. Hopefully, it will lead to a phone, computer, or some way to contact the outside world on the other side.

There are security cameras watching me, but Langston is on a plane right now to God knows where, and Joel is probably passed out drunk on his bed, ignoring me.

I hated growing up with a group of monsters who knew how to hold a gun before they hit puberty. They also knew how to hack security cameras and break into any room.

I jostle the door handle and then insert the bobby pin, easily popping the lock.

I smile slyly when I open the door. I can't believe that Langston didn't use more than a simple lock to keep me out.

My smile is quickly wiped away at my realization. If he was truly hiding something important, something he didn't want me to have, he'd have made it harder.

There is a long hallway before the second half opens up.

I gasp when I see the living space.

It's big and grand—made of marble, quartz, and all the shiny things of a modern fairytale castle. The ceiling on this half of the house is double the height of the other side. The decor is 11th-century castle with a modern touch, not beachy, warm, and full of nature like the rest of the house.

But the biggest difference of all is how dark it is. There are windows, but they are all covered with heavy, black-out curtains. You wouldn't even know you are on the beach in this half of the house.

A woman suddenly appears from deep down the hallway. I didn't hear her because I was too entranced by the house. It's like two houses in one. Two separate lives.

Why did Langston create a house that was half my dream and half this? Whose dream house is this?

The woman folds her arms as she stares at me wordlessly. She has short, choppy hair dyed bright red, so I have no idea what her natural color is. Her skin is toned and unmarked with scars or tattoos. She's wearing a long-sleeved black shirt and dark jeans, not clothes one might wear while living in a beach mansion.

"Phoenix?" I ask, using the name I overheard Langston say.

She stares at me, sizing me up.

"I'm Liesel. I'm wondering if I can borrow your phone?"

On my last syllable, I'm tackled to the ground as if I was aiming a gun at Phoenix's head or something.

"Get off me," I yell as I try to break free of whoever tackled me. It's not Phoenix, she's still standing wordlessly a few feet in front of me.

"Don't move," Joel says. Suddenly, I feel the barrel of a gun against my temple.

I immediately stop moving, stop resisting, and let him pin me to the ground.

"Good girl," Amelia says.

"Amelia?" I glance out of the corner of my eye and see Amelia holding the gun to my head, while Joel applies his full weight to my back.

She smirks at me.

"So, you really aren't a chef?"

"Oh, I can cook. I just also know how to use a weapon."

"Get up," Joel says, yanking me to my feet.

"Is it really necessary to keep pointing that gun at my head?" I snark at Amelia.

She tilts her head. "We were told to keep you out of here at all costs."

I roll my eyes. "You were also told to cook for me, and you were told to keep me safe. You've both already failed."

I look between the two. "And I'm pretty sure if you killed me, Langston wouldn't be too happy. Am I right?"

Joel grabs my hair and sniffs along my neck.

I freeze at his touch, my mind going back to all the times I've been tortured like this.

"Kill me, and Langston will kill you. I'm not afraid of you," I say, keeping my voice calm and steady. They can try to intimidate me all they want, but they can't kill me without dealing with Langston's retaliation.

Joel twists my arm, hard. "We might not be able to kill you, but we sure as hell can punish you for breaking one of Langston's rules."

"Sweet dreams, princess." Amelia hits me hard on the head. It's the last thing I remember.

————

I lift my head and regret it immediately.

My head feels like a knife was jabbed into my forehead and then twisted around.

"Son of a bitch," I groan.

I try to sit up more carefully this time, when I feel the tug of a rope around my wrists.

"Really?"

I glance around the room. I'm in Langston's bed, tied by the wrists to one of the bedposts. Otherwise, the room is empty.

I doubt Langston is back from his expedition, so Joel and Amelia had to be the ones to tie me up.

I take careful inventory of my body as my breathing speeds.

What did they do to me?

I start at my toes and work my way up my body.

No broken bones.

No bruises.

My clothes are still on.

I exhale a heavy breath.

That doesn't mean that they won't do something to me—torture me, rape me.

I have to get out of here.

As much as Langston thinks he has his employees under control, I doubt he told them to knock me out or tie me up. Langston may like to threaten my life, he may torture me, but he's a control freak. He won't like his employees taking matters into their own hands.

I test the rope tying my hands together. It's a good knot—

the person who tied it clearly knows how to tie a knot. But they don't know how to keep a woman like me tied up.

A woman who Langston tied up in the third grade after I stole his favorite Hot Wheels car and threw it in the river. I had rope burn for a week after that. Langston got in so much trouble from his dad. His apology involved teaching me how to get myself out of any binding. We practiced all summer until he could never use that power over me again without me being able to escape.

So untying a sailor's knot is no problem for me. Joel could have made it more difficult if he hadn't used a traditional knot and just tied me up any which way. That would have thrown me for a loop, made it more difficult to undo.

I'm out of the simple knot in three seconds.

I take a second to consider my options. Glancing out the window, the sun is just beginning to set.

I could barricade myself in the bedroom and hope Joel or Amelia don't come check on me, *but how long can I last? How long until Langston comes home?*

No, I don't want to be in this house.

I don't know what Joel and Amelia planned after they tied me up, but I'm not going to wait around to find out. I head to the bathroom balcony and climb over. I scale down the vines, this time with more agility now that I know the easiest path down.

I land on my feet and stare back at the house. Neither Joel nor Amelia come running for me immediately, which gives me time to get away.

I head straight for the ocean. I figure if I run toward the beach, then I can head into the jungle and live off of coconuts until Langston returns and finds me.

I run as fast as I can down the cliffside, so fast that I don't notice her until I'm right on top of her.

Phoenix.

She's sitting in the spot where Langston and I have met every night at sunset.

It's sunset.

There is a bottle of alcohol and two shot glasses sitting next to her.

"Care to join me?" Phoenix asks without glancing back at me.

I raise an eyebrow as I cautiously near her. I wish I had a gun, a weapon, something. She wasn't the one who knocked me out, but she did stand by and watch Joel and Amelia drag me off.

"Who are you?" I ask, standing a few feet away from her instead of sitting down.

"I'm Phoenix; I work for Langston."

"Why do you live in a locked and walled off part of the house?"

Phoenix smiles and looks out to the ocean. "It's part of my job. If I told you, I'd have to kill you."

I shake my head. "That I don't believe. Langston wouldn't allow any of you to kill me. He wants to do that himself."

Phoenix laughs and finally turns to look at me. "That he does, so I think it's best we don't talk about me. That way, neither of us has to kill the other."

"What are you doing?" I nod toward her two glasses of drinks.

"I was instructed to meet you out here every night at sunset, drink a bottle of scotch with you, and try to get you to spill your secrets."

I glance down. "That's a bottle of tequila, not scotch."

She scrunches up her face. "I'm not really a scotch fan, and I don't really plan on getting any secrets out of you. But I figured I should at least attempt to do the job Langston gave me so I don't get fired, unlike those idiots back at the house."

I smirk as I rub the spot where the rope started to dig

into my wrists. "Yea, I'm going to enjoy watching those assholes burn when Langston gets back."

Phoenix grabs the tequila bottle and pours us both a shot.

Then she holds out a glass to me, waiting patiently for me to sit.

"Can you just sit and drink the tequila, so Langston can see that I tried on the security footage?"

"Fine, but only because I want the tequila." I sit down on the sand next to Phoenix, who is still wearing jeans and a long-sleeved T-shirt despite the heat.

I want to be nosy and ask her about it. I want to ask a lot of questions, but based on her appearance, the Langston employee uniform, she must really work for him. My guess is she's a hacker who controls the security cameras. She's probably been watching me this entire time.

Instead of talking, I throw my tequila shot down my throat, enjoying the fiery burn.

"How long have you known Langston?" Phoenix asks me.

I raise an eyebrow as I hold out my glass. She pours me another shot.

Apparently, she doesn't know Langston and I's story. Or if she does, she's playing dumb.

"We met in high school," I lie.

I take the second shot.

"What about you?"

"We've known each other since we were kids," she replies.

I blink rapidly. There is no way Langston has known this woman since they were kids. I knew Langston back then. We used to hang out every day. I would have known this woman, too, if that were true. She's lying just like I am.

"So you go way back. When did you start working for him?"

"Really? We are going to talk about boring topics when we could be trading dirt on Langston?" Phoenix smiles.

"Fine, tell me an embarrassing story from his childhood."

Phoenix's smile falters for just a moment before she starts talking. "We were eight. Langston crashed his bike racing me down a hill. He broke his arm and cried like a baby. I nicknamed him crybaby after that, and I've called him that ever since."

I nod, she's a good liar. She hardly hesitated before launching into the story. It had just enough detail but not too much.

"There's only one little problem with your story," I say.

Phoenix frowns.

"Langston didn't get his first bike until he was twelve. I was there the first day he learned to ride it. He made me hold on to it while he rode it, and when I let go, he fell and skinned both of his knees. And yes, he did cry, but he didn't break an arm. That didn't happen until he was fifteen, was drunk, and fell out of a tree."

Phoenix bites her bottom lip, caught in her lie.

I hold out my drink.

She refills both mine and hers.

I hold out my shot glass. "To being good liars."

She clinks her glass to mine, and we both do the shot together.

"Sorry I lied."

"I'm not. And I'm glad I'm not the only one who thinks Langston is a crybaby."

We both start laughing.

"He's also a control freak," she says.

"A sadistic bastard."

"Fucking secretive asshole."

"An obnoxious liar."

We give each other a knowing look.

"But hot as hell," we both say at the same time before cracking up laughing again. It's probably the tequila warming me to Phoenix. I don't have girlfriends; I don't even have girls that I like. My only friends have been boys. *So why do I feel an instant connection to Phoenix? Like in a different life, we could have been best friends?*

"You ever slept with him?" I ask, jealousy hanging in the air.

"You think I'm going to answer that question honestly?"

I sigh. "Nope. I wouldn't either."

We both sit silently after that.

I don't gain any answers about who Phoenix is. I don't know if she's on my side or not. I don't know anything about her, but I feel a strange connection to my soul. The fact that we can sit silently under the stars, having just met and it not be awkward, tells me all I need to know.

Phoenix isn't being honest. She's a pretty good liar. And yet, she might be the one person in this house who could save me. She might be the key to me getting off this island alive.

I just have to figure out how.

"Liesel, I think—"

"Move, and I'll shoot you," Joel says, interrupting Phoenix.

I freeze, assuming a gun is pointed at the back of my head.

"I'm here talking with Phoenix under Langston's orders. I'm not going anywhere. The gun isn't necessary. I'll lock myself up in my closet for the night, so leave me alone."

"I don't think so. You're a conniving bitch. Langston put me in charge of security. You broke in where you weren't supposed to go. I think I'll use extra rope this time," Joel says.

"Is that really necessary?" Phoenix says, standing and turning around to face Joel.

I, carefully, stand too with hands raised in surrender.

"Yes. You don't know who Liesel is, what she's done. If you did, you'd agree with me, Phoenix."

Phoenix looks at me with new eyes, seeing the monster that I am.

"Shoot me, Joel. If you think I'm so awful, just shoot me. There is no way I'm going to let you tie me up," I say. And then I run.

I run until I feel the sting of a bullet in my shoulder.

LANGSTON

"WHAT'S the plan to get Siren?" I ask as I walk into Zeke's house without saying hello.

"We don't have a plan yet. We don't have any leads. There has been no ransom, no security feed. We don't have any current known enemies," Zeke says.

I could kill Zeke for letting Siren get kidnapped like this. They've been married, what—less than a year, and he's already failed at protecting her.

"You have one job as her husband," I say through gritted teeth.

"Don't lecture me, asshole. Why do you think I called you and Enzo?"

I look past Zeke and see Enzo using a laptop on the kitchen counter, already searching for a clue as to where Siren might have been kidnapped.

"Where's Kai?" I ask.

"She has all the kids in a safehouse with Beckett," Enzo answers.

"Good, now move and let the master work," I say, pushing Enzo off the barstool so I can sit behind the computer.

Enzo doesn't complain. He knows I'm the best behind a computer. I can hack any system, find any missing person.

"Where was Siren last seen?" I ask Zeke.

Zeke runs his hand through his ridiculously long hair while he paces back and forth.

"Zeke!" I growl.

His head snaps to me.

"Focus. Where was Siren last seen?"

"I, uh, I don't know. She told me she had some errands to run. She told me she would pick up Cayden from the nanny and meet me for dinner."

"What errands?"

Zeke shrugs. "I don't know. She didn't tell me. I didn't think to ask."

My eyes flick to Enzo, and we exchange annoyed looks.

I start typing into the computer, searching for Siren's cell phone.

"Her cell phone is turned off," I say a second later.

"Where is the nanny's house?"

"South Beach," Zeke says.

I start there and then expand my search, but as Zeke said, there is no sign of her at the nanny's.

I start searching through the main streets of Miami, searching for a sign of her or her car.

"Wait—her car was last seen at the corner of 15th and Drexel," I say.

Zeke and Enzo both crowd around the computer. We have hope. We are going to be able to find her.

The crank of the garage door fills the silence.

I look from Zeke to Enzo. "Are we expecting anyone else?"

Both men draw their guns in response.

I take a step back from the computer and draw mine as well.

We all aim our guns at the back door as footsteps approach.

The doorknob turns.

And then the door opens.

"Siren," Zeke exhales, dropping his gun and running to her. He grabs her and takes her in his arms. He squeezes her tightly then quickly looks her over for any injuries. He finds none.

"What's going on, guys?" Siren asks, stepping further into the room.

Enzo offers her a quick hug. "I need to go tell Kai you're okay." And then he walks out the door. He's a bit rattled, but he doesn't let anyone see that.

Siren looks to me, and then she runs into my arms. I squeeze her as tightly as Zeke did.

"Don't do that to me, Ren," I whisper into her ear, tears threatening at the fear of losing her.

"Do what? Get a flat tire while I was out shopping for my husband and let my phone die? That?"

"Yea, don't do that. Don't make me install a tracker in you so I never lose you again."

She smiles. "You'll never lose me."

I nod.

"Can I talk to my wife alone now?" Zeke asks, giving me a grumpy stare.

I roll my eyes. "She might be your wife, but she's my friend."

Zeke grabs Siren's hand, and she winks at me. "Be back soon," she whispers as Zeke pulls her upstairs to most likely fuck her brains out and remind her she's his.

I find the liquor cabinet and pour myself a drink before walking outside to the deck that overlooks the beach.

I sit outside, alone for a while with my thoughts. None of them are about Siren, only Liesel.

"Care to tell your best friend what's on your mind?" Siren asks as she steps outside.

"Worried about you," I say.

"Liar." She leans back against the railing, facing me in my chair. "Are you going to tell me the truth, or do I have to beat it out of you?"

I chuckle at that.

"Liesel," I surrender.

"Oh. What's new with Liesel? Did Kai tell you that she's thinking about going on our girl's trip with us in a week?"

"Liesel's not going."

Siren frowns. "Why not?"

"Because I kidnapped her, and I say she's not going."

"You what?" Siren exclaims.

"I kidnapped Liesel. I'm holding her hostage. I threatened to kill her."

"Please tell me this is a joke? That I'm not hearing you correctly?"

"It's not a joke."

"What? Why…? I don't understand."

"It's a long story that I'm not going to get into, but she left me no choice."

"Langston Finn Pearce, you do too have a choice. What the hell? Let her go right now!"

"No."

"Langston? What is your plan?"

"I'm going to get Liesel to talk, and then I'm going to kill her."

Siren gasps. "You're lying. You're not going to kill Liesel. Aren't you, like, in love with her?"

I shake my head. "I was never in love with her."

"Let her go, Langston."

"No."

She shoves me hard. "Let. Her. Go."

"You're not the boss of me." I shove her back.

"What the hell is going on out here?" Zeke sticks his head out.

"My best friend is being an ass. Do something about it for me." Siren throws her hands up.

"What did you do?" Zeke asks.

"I kidnapped Liesel. No big deal. I have everything under control."

Zeke's fist comes flying at my face.

I try to deflect, but my reflexes are slow after all the alcohol, and he hits me in the eye.

"Should I punch him again or is once enough?" Zeke asks Siren.

"I don't know. Do you think kidnapping Liesel and threatening her with death only deserves one punch?" Siren puts her hands on her hips, looking stern.

Zeke punches me again.

"Stop," I say. "You've made your point. And who are you to punch me when you did the same thing to Siren?"

Zeke looks to Siren. "He has a point."

"It's still doesn't make it okay," Siren says.

"Come on, let's go to sleep. We can try to talk some sense into him in the morning," Zeke says, walking back to the door.

Siren nods but stops before going back inside. She looks at me with concern.

"Be careful with Liesel, she's dangerous."

I chuckle. "Liesel is no you, Siren. She's a terrible shot. She's never killed a man. All she knows how to do is hunt and lie. I think I can handle her just fine."

I rush past her to go sleep off my hangover in one of their guest bedrooms.

"That's not what I mean. She has the ability to hurt you in other ways."

"How?"

"Like stealing your heart," Siren smirks and then leaves me all alone.

Siren is wrong, but she is right about one thing—Liesel is dangerous.

2 7

LIESEL

WHEN I WAKE up this time, I already know where I am, and that I'm tied up.

Joel and Amelia are predictable in that way.

This time instead of just my arms, they've tied my legs together too. Thankfully they've tied them together instead of spread apart. I can hope that means that they don't plan on violating me.

I wiggle my wrists, testing my bindings.

"Don't even think about it," Amelia says from the corner of Langston's bedroom.

She stands from the chair she must have brought up and looks down at me with a bored expression. "We tied them with extra rope, and I'm under specific instruction to shoot you again if you move."

Again?

I shift my shoulder slightly, and I feel the burning pang of the bullet lodged in my scapula. I don't let her know how much pain I'm in, though. I'm too stubborn to show any weakness to this woman.

"Under whose instruction?" I ask.

217

"Langston's. I called him and told him you were trying to run. He told me to do whatever it takes to hold you until he returned."

"When is he returning?" I ask.

"He didn't say. But you and I are going to enjoy our time together until he does."

I try to relax. I try to fall back asleep. There is nothing I can do right now but wait until Langston comes back, or at least until Amelia makes a mistake and gives me a chance to escape. All I can do is live with the pain in my shoulder.

There is a knock on the door. My eyes fill with hope for a split second that Langston has returned. I know the bastard wants me dead, but not yet—not for an entire year. Not until he's bled me dry of my secrets. This bitch, Amelia, will kill me without thinking twice about it.

Langston wouldn't knock, though. My hope quickly floats away.

"Yes?" Amelia answers, sounding irritated to be interrupted.

"It's time for a shift change," Phoenix says, walking into the room. Her eyes hold no emotion as she looks at Amelia, acting like I'm not even in the room.

Amelia glances at her watch. "I still have thirty minutes left. And Joel is up next, not you."

"Joel told me he needs you to fix the coffee machine before he goes on shift. He's hungover and showering," Phoenix says.

God, she's a good liar.

"Fine. Do you have a weapon? This one needs it to make her obey. We tied her up with extra rope this time, but somehow the bitch figured out how to untangle herself last time."

Phoenix eyes the gun in Amelia's hand. "I'm good."

Amelia nods. "Call me if you have any trouble."

And then Amelia leaves.

Phoenix stands quietly in place. I'm not sure what she's doing, but then I notice that her eyes are closed. She's listening.

I close my eyes too, and hear Amelia's footsteps downstairs.

"We don't have much time," Phoenix says, running to me and going to work on my wrists.

"No, start with my ankles, I can do my wrists."

"There are too many ropes; there is no way you can untie yourself. If I can get your arms free, then you can help with your ankles."

"Trust me, work on my ankles."

Phoenix hesitates for a second, but I nod my encouragement.

"Okay," she relents and moves to my ankles.

I start working on my wrists.

"The coffee machine needs fixing, huh? That's probably because you were the one who broke it," Joel says from the doorway.

We both freeze.

"Shit," Phoenix mutters under her breath.

She turns and looks at him. "I was just making sure you tied these ropes tight enough so she doesn't get away this time."

"Uh, huh. Sure, you were. Get back to your half to the house and leave this to us."

"But—" Phoenix starts.

"Now," Joel grows.

Phoenix flashes me a look of apology. There is a guilty sadness in her eyes. She knows what happens next, and there is nothing she can do about it.

I smile. "It's okay, go," I whisper so only she can hear. My voice is full of strength.

Phoenix bites her lip, clearly concerned, but her staying won't stop this. She doesn't have a weapon; she's not like Amelia, who has clearly had combat training. I don't know what role Phoenix plays yet, but my guess is some kind of IT role that helps manage the computers and security systems. An important role, but useless right now. If she stays, she'll just end up beaten as well.

"Go," I nod.

Phoenix gives me a stubborn look, and I think she might stay, but at the last second, she turns and leaves without a word.

As soon as Phoenix walks out the door, Joel slams it shut and flicks the lock.

He looks at me with a sadistic grin. His eyes turn fiery, and he cracks his knuckles, preparing to hurt me.

"If you touch me, Langston is going to kill you," I say, warning him.

He laughs. "You still think after everything Langston has done to you that he cares about you?"

No, Langston doesn't care about me. Not anymore. But he wants information from me. And he doesn't like sharing me while he waits for me to spill my guts.

"Yes," I lie.

That makes Joel laugh harder as he walks toward my prison bed.

My wrists are tied together and then to the headboard just like before. My ankles are bound, but not to anything else. I can move my legs, just as one unit.

Joel eyes my legs.

"Kick me, and I'll shoot you again," Joel says, pulling his gun out and aiming at me.

I force my legs to remain still.

"I thought Amelia was the one who shot me?"

"Nope, I did. Amelia doesn't have the guts I do."

I'm sure.

Slowly, with his gun pointed at my chest, Joel climbs onto the bed and then eventually straddles me until he's crushing my stomach with his weight. My legs are now basically useless. I could kick him in the back, but not hard enough to force him off me.

He grabs my chin and holds me still, lowering his head toward mine.

"Langston is going to kill you," I say again.

"Keep dreaming." Joel forces a slobbery kiss onto my lips.

I try to squirm away, but he's stronger.

He chuckles. "What? You don't like that? You didn't seem to mind before."

Wait...before?

I search my mind. *Did he rape me last time I was tied up?*

He laughs at my quizzical expression and then holds up a finger to my lips.

"That's right. You enjoyed my fingers in your cunt. This time, you're going to enjoy my cock."

Oh.

My.

God.

It was Joel whose fingers I rode, not Langston. *Was it Joel's cock that I fucked too?*

I squirm hard, my fingers going to work to untie myself. The pain in my shoulder is exploding with every move, but I won't let this man touch me.

"Langston's going to kill you!" I yell.

Joel slaps me hard across the cheek, the sting making me stop squirming long enough for his words to land.

"Langston was the one who told me to do my worst that night. He doesn't care what I do to you. He's just using you, and as soon as you are no longer useful to him, he'll dispose of you."

Joel's words impact me more forcefully than the bullet in my shoulder. I thought I was safe with Langston. I thought he would protect me. I thought…

Everything I thought was wrong.

I'm on my own.

Langston won't protect me.

The epiphany makes me fight like hell.

Joel leans in to kiss me again, and this time, I open my mouth, enticing his tongue deep into my orifice. Then, I enjoy biting down as wickedly as I can on his tongue.

I feel the iron taste of blood in my mouth and hear the high pitched squeal of pain leaving Joel's throat. In response, I bite down harder.

Joel is smarter than I give him credit for, though. He punches me hard in the stomach, making me gasp for air, releasing his tongue.

I'm rewarded with the sight of blood covering the bastard's mouth. I got him good.

His face turns sinister, his eyes swirl in evil circles, a vein bulges in his forehead, and his mouth growls like a bear.

I injured him, and that pissed him off. He's going to try and take his fury out on me, but it still won't stop me from fighting.

"You fucking cunt! You bit me!" he roars.

He grabs my shoulders, one hand digging into the back of my shoulder on my gunshot wound.

The pain bolts down my arm excruciatingly, races down my back, and crashes in my head. My body is firing off a million nerve endings all at once, telling me to run, to get away from this man. He will destroy me if I don't stop him.

I refuse to scream, to cry out.

He smirks. "You think you're a tough woman? Don't worry, I can do this all day. Eventually, I will get your screams."

He grabs for my jeans shorts and starts shoving them down my body.

I know what comes next.

And I can't take it.

I try to headbutt him, but I miss.

I frantically try to untangle my wrists, but he notices and holds onto my hands with one of his large, dirty mitts while the other shoves unwanted into my panties.

I cringe and turn my face away, so he can't see the suffering he's causing me. I won't let him have my pain, my fear, my agony. That I will keep to myself. If I can't beat him, I at least won't give him what he wants. That's how I survived Enzo's father. That's how I'll survive this scumbag too.

A throat clears, and my head snaps in the direction of the door.

Joel hears it too. His fingers stop fumbling in my bikini bottoms. Slowly and carefully, he removes his hand, trying to hide his actions from the voice at the door.

"You're back early, sir. I was just teaching Miss Dunn a lesson in what happens to thieves on this island," Joel says, his head looking over his shoulder at Langston, while continuing to straddle my body.

Liar. I didn't steal anything.

"I can see that," Langston answers, his voice low and orderly. He doesn't seem upset at all to find Joel groping me.

Joel was right, Langston doesn't care about me.

Langston doesn't look at me; he only looks at Joel.

"I can handle Miss Dunn from here. Thank you, Joel."

"Yes, sir." Joel smirks at me and then rolls off me before exiting the room.

Then it's just Langston and me.

I'm still tied up. My face is covered in Joel's blood.

Surprisingly, my shoulder has little blood on it. I doubt he even realizes I'm bleeding from a gunshot wound.

Langston doesn't say anything. He just studies me a second, taking in the scene. I take the moment to study him.

He's wearing jeans and a grey V-neck. He looks the same, but I see the bruises around his eye. Whatever he went and did, he got at least once punch for it. There are probably more beneath his shirt.

"Can you untie yourself?" he asks.

My eyes narrow. "Yes."

"Good."

And then Langston turns and walks out of the room.

That's it? That's all Langston is going to say or do?

Now, I'm pissed. He didn't even ask what happened or check if I'm injured, check to see what Joel did to me.

Langston really does hate me.

His hate motivates me to untie myself faster.

I had already made progress on my wrists, so I finish them quickly and start on my ankles. I fumble once or twice before finally freeing myself.

I pull my jean shorts back up and then head to the bathroom. I wipe the blood from my face on Langston's white towels, happy to be ruining them. I can't reach my wound, and I don't want to look at how violently my shoulder is fucked up.

I rummage for some painkillers and find none.

Dammit.

I run my hand through my blonde wavy hair. I'm strong. I'm going to go kick Langston's ass and demand painkillers and a doctor. Then I'm going to find a way off this mother-fucking island.

I consider my options: walk down the stairs or climb down the vines.

I choose vines.

It takes everything in me to climb down the wall, basically one-handed. My left shoulder is useless with the bullet lodged in it, but finally, my feet hit the ground.

I sneak around the house, keeping my head low to avoid being seen out the windows as I look for Langston.

I make it to the front of the house before I hear voices.

"I told you not to touch her," Langston says, he has a gun pointed at Joel's head, and Joel is kneeling in front of him.

My eyes widen. *I was right, not Joel.*

Amelia is standing off to the side with tears in her eyes.

"You didn't listen. You touched her that first night when I told you not to. I told you to just scare her a bit. And what the hell was that I just walked in on?"

"She broke into the half of the house that was off-limits, sir. She was trying to run. She—" Joel says.

"No, I pay you to prevent that. She shouldn't have been able to escape in the first place if you were doing your job. And you sure as hell aren't allowed to touch her."

"I'm sorry. I—" Joel says.

Langston doesn't let him finish his sentence. He shoots Joel square in the forehead. His body drops lifelessly to the ground.

I gasp but snap my hands quickly over my mouth so Langston doesn't know that I'm watching him.

Amelia holds her hands up as Langston aims the gun at her. "Please, I'm so sorry. It will never happen again."

"I'm only letting you live because I don't want to deal with the body. Get rid of him and then get off my fucking island. If I ever see your face again, Amelia, I'll kill you, too."

Amelia nods, tears streaming down her face now.

I slink away from the window and along the house.

I can't believe what I just saw. Maybe I wasn't so wrong about Langston after all.

I stop to dart into the kitchen and find a bottle of scotch

and a towel, quickly running back outside. I don't know what to make of everything that just happened. I need some space to decompress everything. The scotch will help with the pain until I'm ready to face Langston again.

What are you up to, Langston?

I always thought I was the only one with secrets. I thought his only secrets were the contents of the half of my letter he stole. Now, I'm beginning to think he has secrets of his own.

28

LANGSTON

IT'S BEEN a long time since I've felt this level of anger.

I thought shooting Joel would dissipate some of it, but I'm more pissed off than I was when I first caught them.

I can't trust any of my employees.

I've always known that. The only way you gain the kind of trust required to do this job is by working side by side, battling for your lives and growing up together. The kind of trust that I have with Enzo and Zeke. That's not possible with any of my employees.

I have money, but I'm not filthy rich like Enzo. I can pay my employees well, but not well enough to ensure they are loyal. And the threat of death only goes so far. I'm guessing now that I've killed one of them, the rest will be more likely to stay in line.

God, I can't get the images out of my head.

I was still in the air, about an hour out, when the security feed came through. I just wanted to see Liesel, see what she was up to. That's when I found her tied to my bed.

She looked dead, but I couldn't see any bullet or stab wounds, no blood.

I implored my pilot to fly faster, but we weren't fast enough.

As soon as I landed, I drove like a maniac to get here. I didn't trust anyone to stop what was happening. And then I saw Joel enter the room.

Up to that point, Liesel was just tied up. I could think of a million ways my huntress could have gotten herself into that position. A billion tricks she could have pulled on my staff that made them think she was a vicious creature needing to be tied up.

Joel climbed on top of her.

He kissed what is mine!

And he said he had violated her before.

I became a bull about to ram through everyone in my way at that point.

I couldn't watch the rest, and yet I couldn't drag my eyes away.

I watched as she drew blood.

I watched as she struggled to free herself.

I watched her stronger than I've ever seen her, not making a single sound of pain, fear, or defeat. It's then that I realized my entire strategy had been wrong. There is no way I'm breaking Liesel. She's too durable, impenetrable.

But if anyone is going to break her, it's going to be me.

When I finally got here, it took all of my control not to show her how I felt. I was the one breaking for her. I've always been breaking for her.

I ordered Joel away.

Even then, it took everything in me to walk away from her. We both needed space. She deserved space to hate me for failing her again.

After shooting Joel, I probably should have killed Amelia too, but I didn't want to spend the day getting rid of two dead bodies.

Instead, I spent the day giving Liesel space. I spent it trying to put the fear of God into the rest of my team, laying down rules and making it perfectly clear what will happen if they lay a finger on Liesel without my permission.

I pick out a new man as my head of security to replace Joel. Unfortunately, no one else on the team is a good cook, so we will be chefless for the time being.

All I know is that I don't trust a damn soul on this island —not even Phoenix, who has decided to give me the silent treatment today.

As for Liesel, she's been at the beach all day.

I gave her her space. I needed it as much as she did.

But the sun is setting—it's time to talk.

I grab the most expensive bottle of scotch I own. One I don't think Liesel has tried, but she'll love. I carry it and two glasses down the sandy cove to the beach.

Liesel is sitting in our spot in the sand already. I'm pretty sure she's sat here all day. She has a towel wrapped around her like she's cold, but the sun's heat is still beating on us. I'm sweating as I walk, so there is no way she's cold.

Then I spot the bottle she's lifting to her lips. It only has a fourth of the liquid left in it. She's probably drunk off her ass if that bottle was full when she started this morning. She's trying to chase her demons away with alcohol, trying to chase away Joel. She doesn't know that he's already paid for what he did to her.

I sit down next to her in the sand.

She doesn't look over at me, just brings the bottle back to her lips.

"Where's Joel?" she asks with surprising clarity for a woman who spent the day drinking.

"He quit."

"Uh-huh," she says, not believing me.

"You don't have to worry about Joel anymore."

"I know."

I frown, not sure what she means. She's drunk, so I'm not going to get any clear answers from her tonight. Tonight is just about getting back into our routine.

"I told you not to trust anyone but me," I say.

"Oh, so this is my fault?" Her head snaps to me with the venom of a cobra as she looks at me.

Her towel drops away as she snarls at me, and my world freezes.

Blood.

Dried blood covers her shoulder.

I think back to Joel. I don't remember him having any wound except for his tongue, where she bit him. And of course, the giant hole I put in his head.

I reach out to examine her shoulder, but Liesel pulls away, re-covering herself with the towel.

That's why she has the towel: to hide her pain.

"Liesel, let me see your shoulder," I say calmly and firmly. I won't give her a choice in the matter. I need to see her injuries, but I won't physically force her.

Her eyes tear into me, and once again, she looks ready to strike.

"Please," I force my voice to soften.

She blinks rapidly, trying to find a way out of showing me her shoulder. Eventually, something she sees in my eyes forces her to let me.

She nods and relinquishes her hold on the towel, but doesn't remove it herself.

I reach out, and she doesn't pull away this time.

I grab the towel, preparing myself not to react to what-ever I see.

When I lower the towel, I see the dried blood once again, and then I see the gaping hole blasted into the back of her shoulder.

A bullet hole.

In the back.

The fucking bastard shot her running away. He didn't even have the decency to shoot her face to face.

"Shit," I curse, grinding my teeth together.

Liesel's hazel eyes water, but she doesn't cry.

Once again, I failed her. I should have been here instead of searching for Siren. I should have known Joel was a bastard. I should have known she'd been shot.

And I shouldn't be showing her any damn emotion, but there is no hiding how I feel.

I pull the rest of the towel from her back, examining every inch of her with my own eyes, but I only see the single bullet hole.

"Joel did this?"

Liesel nods.

"Did he hurt you anywhere else?"

Please, don't tell me he raped you and I didn't realize.

"No, you got here before he could do worse."

I narrow my gaze; my heart roars in my chest full of a thousand exploding angry cannons. I didn't get here in time. He should have never touched her. Never tied her up. Never shot her.

I regret killing the bastard now—he deserved worse than death.

"Hold this," I say, handing Liesel the expensive bottle of scotch.

She leaves her bottle in the sand and takes mine in her arms, cradling it against her chest.

Then, I scoop her up in my arms, lifting her as gently as I can. She hisses when I first touch her, but something in my eyes must convince her to not fight me.

I carry her back into the house and up to my bedroom

before realizing that putting her back in the bed where she was tied up and almost raped probably isn't the best idea.

"It's okay," Liesel says when I start to turn back.

"You sure?"

She nods.

I set her gently on the edge of the bed, and then I run to the bathroom, popping open a panel in the wall where I keep my emergency supplies. I grab the first aid kit. It's more like a wound healer kit, though. The only thing the kit is good for is dealing with bullet or knife wounds.

I carry the bag out and set it on the bed. Then I take the scotch bottle from her and set it on the nightstand. My eyes don't leave her now. I can't stop looking at her.

"Do you want me to call a doctor or do you want—"

"You—I want you to do it."

I nod.

"Painkillers or more scotch?"

The corner of her mouth lifts at that. "What do you think?"

I smile lightly and grab the bottle of scotch from the nightstand. It's the most expensive bottle in the house, over $30K. This isn't exactly the situation I imagined using it on. She's not going to take the time to savor the thick peat and sherry cask finish.

But right now, I'd give Liesel the world if I could.

I pop the bottle open and take a quick sip myself to steady my nerves before I handle it to her. She takes it, but I realize now it's a mistake. The bottle is heavy and hard to lift with her injured shoulder.

I hold the base and help lift it to her lips. I keep holding it until she gets enough down to ease her pain.

When I remove the bottle and set it back on the night-stand, she lifts an eyebrow. "I may already be drunk, but that was the best damn scotch I've ever tasted."

I smirk. "Don't get used to it. That's a thirty thousand dollar bottle."

Her eyebrows shoot up. "If you're paying, I could definitely get used to it."

I shake my head and then move closer to the bed.

"I'm going to sit behind you so I can get the bullet out, okay?"

She nods.

I've removed plenty of bullets before—out of my buddies, my coworkers, my employees, but never out of Liesel.

I gather my supplies, trying to think of her like any other person, but as I hold the tweezers up to her back, I hesitate.

"Oh, don't puss out on me now. If you can't pull a bullet out of my back, how am I supposed to believe that you're going to kill me?" Liesel teases.

But I hear the underlying fear. She knows there is a difference between hurting and killing her. When you kill someone, you don't have to deal with their pain and agony. Pulling this out is going to hurt like a motherfucker. I know, I have scars all over my body to prove it.

"Hold still. Scream, yell, cry if you have to, just don't move, understand?"

"Yes," she hisses.

I wish I could hold her hand as I do this. Not that that really helps, but at least I'd feel like I was doing something for her.

I push the tweezers in, digging for the bullet.

She doesn't move.

She doesn't hiss.

Scream.

Cry.

Did she pass out from the pain? Die of a sudden heart attack?

No, she's still breathing.

"Will you hurry up? This isn't exactly enjoyable for me, you know?"

I laugh. "Deep breath, Liesel."

And then I yank the bullet out on her exhale.

I plop the bullet and tweezers into a plastic bag and then apply gauze to her shoulder to stop the bleeding.

"Hard part's over."

"Really? I imagine the stitches aren't a cakewalk."

"Staples are faster."

"Let's go with the staples then," Liesel says, flashing me a grin over her shoulder.

I grab the bottle of scotch and hold it up to her lips. "Take one more sip."

She grips the bottle with her good arm and starts drinking while I apply the three quick staples into her back. Then I secure a gauze bandage to the wound and wipe the blood from her back and arm.

"All done," I say.

She nods and rests the bottle between her legs on the bed.

I gather up the supplies, put them back in the bag, and carry them into the bathroom, where I catch a glance of myself in the mirror.

I'm a monster.

She deserves better.

When I walk back into the bedroom, I lock eyes with her.

Liesel—the badass motherfucker.

My huntress.

My liar.

Mine.

I won't fail you again.

And to prove it, I say two little words I never thought I'd say to her.

"I'm sorry."

29

LIESEL

Langston apologized.

I don't know what to do with that.

"Need anything else? Can I get you more painkillers? Food? Anything?" Langston asks.

I'm still sitting on the edge of the bed, and he's standing just inside the room looking like someone stole his puppy, and he got into a fistfight.

"Ice," I answer.

He nods and then jogs out of the room.

It gives me a moment, but there is too much to process.

My shoulder throbs, although not as painfully as before. The alcohol is numbing the most intense suffering.

It did hurt like hell when he dug the bullet out, though. I refused to show weakness, especially in front of Langston, my killer.

Is he still going to kill me?

He hesitated to pull the bullet out. It was as difficult for him as it was for me.

A lot can change in a year which, give or take a few weeks, is what I have left. That's the timeline he gave me.

One year.

I can get him to change his mind in a year. Get him to warm to me again like when we were kids. Get him to feel things so he can't fathom killing me.

Langston is back.

"Do you want to move to another bedroom?" he asks. It's clear he's worried that I'll have nightmares about being tied up and almost raped if we stay in here.

I shake my head. "That's not how my nightmares work."

He enters, carrying a bag of ice and a bowl of something with two spoons sticking out.

"Climb under the covers and sit back in the bed," he orders.

I do.

He plops the bowl down in my lap and then puts the bag of ice on my shoulder. Finally, he climbs into the bed next to me. He sits on top of the covers, while I sit under.

He brought me a bowl of buttered pecan ice cream—my favorite.

"You should have more than just scotch in your belly."

I smile lightly; I can't help it.

"What's the second spoon for?"

"Me." He takes a bite of my ice cream before I can jerk the bowl out of his reach.

That makes us both laugh. We both need a laugh, even if it doesn't make sense.

"Here," I say, reaching behind my shoulder to grab the bag of ice and toss it at him.

"What's this for?"

"Your eye—it looks terrible. And if I know you, you didn't ice it at all today. You might need your eye to be able to see and shit."

"I think your shoulder needs it more."

"Nope." I grab the bottle of scotch. "This is all my shoulder needs."

He doesn't argue with me, probably because he feels guilty. He just puts the ice to his swollen eye.

Progress.

I smile to myself as I take a bite of the heavenly ice cream.

"I haven't told you my story for the night," I say after taking a few more bites.

"I'll give you a pass for tonight, since you were shot and all."

"You're not getting out of story time with me that easily."

"Story time with you? I thought I was the one torturing you by making you tell me stories."

I put the spoon in my mouth and scrape the ice cream off with my teeth.

Langston stares at me like he's entranced with my mouth, wishing he was my spoon right now.

"Nope, story time is about putting tiny little cuts into your heart every single night. I can't kill you with one big blow, but I can kill you if I inflict enough scratches."

"Okay, what story are you going to tell me tonight?" He leans back, resting his head on the headboard. He holds the ice to his eye, and I hold my spoon of ice cream up to his lips.

He hesitantly takes a bite. Now I'm the one who can't stop staring at his lips.

"Liesel? Are you going to tell me a story or not? It's been a long day, and I'd like to sleep at some point." He says it like he's irritated with me, but we both know it's out of concern for me. He's just looking out for me, making sure that I get sleep, which is the best thing for my shoulder.

Rest and time are the only things that will heal it now.

I lean back too, trying not to wince when my shoulder hits the headboard.

"I think we were twelve or thirteen; I can't remember the

exact year. That doesn't really matter, anyway. You had just kissed Ruby."

"Thirteen. I was thirteen."

I hit his shoulder playfully. "Of course, you would remember how old you were when you kissed Ruby."

"Wouldn't you?"

I hem and haw. "Yea, probably. No more interrupting my story."

He gestures to zipper his mouth shut.

I smile and get distracted by his adorable dimple.

No—focus.

"You and I rode our bikes together on the way home from school. I saw you kissing her earlier that day, and I teased you the whole way home."

Langston's face drops as he realizes the story I'm going to tell, but he's not sure why I chose it.

"We got to your house, and I kept teasing you, even though I saw your father drinking beer in his chair. Even though I knew not to be loud. Even though I knew not to tease you about something your father wouldn't approve."

"Liesel," Langston says in a warning tone.

I keep going.

"I knew what was going to happen, and I kept pushing, teasing. I was jealous that you kissed that girl. And I wanted to make you pay."

Langston's eyes close, as if remembering.

"Your father beat you, and it was my fault. I provoked him. I knew you got beat every time he was triggered, and I did nothing."

I reach up and touch his face.

He opens his eyes.

When he looks at me, he knows why I told this story. Every time he gets hit, it reminds him of his father. And I'm still sorry for not saving him when we were kids.

"I'll go sleep in the closet," I say, moving to get up.

Langston grabs my wrist, stopping me.

"Liar."

"What?"

"You're a liar."

I frown. "What part of that story was a lie? You lived that story with me. Every word was the truth."

He removes the ice from his face and looks at me with both eyes.

"You did do something to stop him, Liesel."

How does he know?

"You did something every time you could. You told my mother. You tried to calm him down or get him extra drunk so that he wouldn't be able to hit me."

He's right. I did. I just never realized that Langston knew that.

"But that night—"

He puts a finger to my lips, getting me to stop.

"You took a beating for me."

I freeze, and my eyes widen. *How did he know?*

He nods as if my reaction confirms it. He didn't know for sure until this very moment.

Langston gets up out of bed and turns off the lights.

I feel him return a moment later.

He climbs into the bed, this time under the covers.

"Go to sleep, Liesel."

This time he doesn't give me a choice between the closet or his bed; he demands I sleep in his bed. For the first time since I slept next to him when we were kids, I want to share a bed with him.

30

LANGSTON

"Please."

The single word stirs me awake.

I'm a light sleeper. It's one of the many reasons why I excel at security and protecting people—well, protecting everyone other than Liesel.

My eyes fly open and look to the woman lying on my shoulder.

Liesel Dunn.

Her head is snuggled up against my bare chest.

"Please," she whimpers again.

"Shh, I got you," I whisper into her ear, but I don't think she's actually awake. She's just having a dream or, most likely, a nightmare.

I feel her forehead—it's covered in sweat. Her body trembles in my arms. She feels like an addict in need of her next fix.

I've had my suspicions of what her demons actually are ever since she arrived. Holding her while she sleeps seems to confirm them.

"I need you, please," Liesel whispers again, her hands start clawing at my chest.

"Liesel," I say, freezing.

Her thigh drapes over mine, and she starts humping my leg, moving her body over mine like she's desperate.

"Liesel, wake up." I stroke her hair.

"Please, make me come. I need it."

She tries again to rub herself against me. To feel something. To let go. But she can't.

Suddenly, the dream shifts.

"Get off of me!"

She's no longer begging for my body but begging me to let her go.

Her fists slam against my chest, over and over. Her body somehow heats to an even higher temperature. She has to be running a fever. She has to be having a nightmare.

"Let me go!" she yells.

Now I'm not sure if she's awake or asleep, but I can't let her go. If I let her go, she'll run. She'll hurt herself—her shoulder.

"Liesel, wake up."

"Let me go!" Her legs start kicking. She's terrified.

I don't know what to do.

I don't know how to help her.

"Please," her mood shifts again, and this time she's begging.

I don't know what to do.

I don't know where my brain goes or why I think this is a good idea.

I roll her onto her back and hover an inch over her.

I kiss her.

The second our lips touch, her eyes open.

I should stop the kiss.

I should pull away.

I don't.

And she doesn't push me away.

So I savor the moment. This kiss won't be repeated. This kiss tastes just like I always thought it would. Sure, I kissed her when we were kids, but that was before I knew how to actually kiss.

This kiss, I take everything I can.

I feel the soft warmth of her lips.

I plunge my tongue into her depths, finding hers and dancing with it, already knowing her next move. Her tongue is going to battle mine for control. I expect to feel frustrated that she doesn't just resign to me.

Instead, I feel like she woke a hurricane of emotions inside me. I feel the sparks, the electricity, the waves crashing between us.

I would say I didn't expect this—but that would be a lie. It's one of the reasons I haven't kissed her until now. Until I felt like I didn't have a choice.

Liesel grabs the back of my head when I start to pull away.

There's a pause, and then I attack her with my kisses. I can't control myself. I can't think. I want to drown in her kisses.

I shouldn't. This is wrong for so many reasons.

I'm destroying everything I've worked for with one stupid kiss.

But damn, this kiss is worth it.

Suddenly, the intensity of it all becomes too much. Like two spark plugs forced together, the zap eventually pushes us apart as much as it pulled us together at first.

We both pant heavily.

"That was our first kiss?" she says like it's a question.

"Yes, if you don't count that kiss when we were eight."

"I don't."

I nod in agreement. That was nothing like this kiss.

"You've never fucked me?" she asks. She's just now figuring out the truth.

I shake my head.

"You've never fingered me?"

I shake my head.

"Never done anything sexual with me?"

I shake my head.

"Oh my god, then who did?"

"Mostly hallucinations in your nightmares."

She holds onto her shirt, gripping for reality, for truth.

"Joel?" she asks, her voice terrified of my answer.

"No," I lie. I failed to protect her before, but dammit, I'll protect her now. She never has to know about Joel.

But the rest?

The rest of the truth, I'll take to my grave.

31

LIESEL

THAT KISS.

That kiss was terrifying, breathtaking.

It also brought me back to life.

It changed how I felt about Langston. Or maybe it brought me back to how I once felt?

I want to kiss him again.

And yet, if I kiss him again, I'll ruin everything.

But did he ruin everything already?

Is he lying?

He said we never fucked, he never touched me, and that Joel didn't touch me. *Is it true? Or is it all a lie?*

I trust him.

It doesn't matter if it's the truth or a lie. It's what I need to hear.

I'm a sex addict. I use sex to deal with the pain of my past.

But god, that kiss—do I wish I could have more than one.

That's what I think about as I drift back to sleep. It's what I think about all night. That kiss is still playing on my lips in the morning when I wake up.

"Langston?" I ask to an empty room as the sun rises.

I get no answer.

The room is bright. Maybe I slept in too long, and that's why he's not here.

Or maybe I scared him off last night.

Maybe he's changed his mind and wants to end my life sooner than planned.

I sit up, my body aching with pain. I need more painkillers or more scotch.

I reach for the scotch bottle next to the bed and see that it's been replaced with a bottle of painkillers and a glass of water.

"Fine," I say, resigning myself to meds instead of alcohol to deal today.

I pop two pills and drink the water.

Then I get out of bed. I consider showering or soaking in the tub, but I want to find Langston.

So I just head downstairs, feeling much happier and lighter than I should.

The house is quiet as I hit the bottom step.

I decide to grab a coffee before I continue my search. The pot is still on, and there is enough for one cup left. I pour myself a cup, happily humming a song in my head when my world stops.

I look out the big glass doors that are usually open to the outside by now, but I'm guessing that was Amelia's job. No one else has gotten into a routine to open the house up yet.

It's not the closed doors causing my heart to skip—it's what I see just beyond them.

Langston kissing Phoenix.

Not a chicken peck either, a full-on slam me against the wall and take my breath away kind of kiss. The kind that you get swept up in and don't notice the world around you. I know what kissing Langston like that feels like. I experienced it last night.

And now he's kissing Phoenix.

They don't notice me. *How could they, locked in a lip battle like that?*

I have two choices—go back to Langston's room and pretend I didn't see them, biding my time until I bring the subject up, or make it clear that I see them and I'm pissed.

I'm usually pretty good with self-control. Not today.

Coffee still in hand, I storm through the glass doors, making my presence as obvious as possible. They can't hide what I saw.

They both stop at the sound of the door swinging open. Or maybe it's my stomping and the fire shooting from my body that drew their attention my way, but they don't separate. Phoenix still clings to Langston's arm.

"So you're not only a liar; you're also a cheater," I say, glaring at Langston. Phoenix, I can't really be mad at. I thought she was my friend, but then I've only known her for a couple of days. I can't be upset with her. Langston, on the other hand, I want to bury with the fires of hell.

I want to fight. I want to knee Langston in the groin. I want to run him off a cliff.

But I know that not doing any of those things is more powerful. He knows I'm pissed, and now he has to wait to see what my next move will be and when I'll make it.

I walk past them and head to the beach, wishing I had something stronger than coffee in my hand. I plop down on the sandy beach with the sun beating down on me. My hot coffee isn't going to do much to help with the sweltering sun. Soon, I'll have to go back and get water, or at least find a shady spot to sit.

"I'm not a cheater," Langston says from behind me.

I snap my head. "Oh, really? What would you call kissing me while you're dating her? I'm pretty sure most people would classify that as cheating."

"I only kissed you to get you to stop having your night-mares." Langston's hands are in the pockets of his swim trunks, and he's wearing a plain white T-shirt. He looks like the boy I used to know before Enzo sunk his claws into him. He looks light and carefree, but I can see the turmoil in his eyes.

I nod and glance away. He's right. He only kissed me to help me. All the rest was just my imagination. Langston didn't touch me; he didn't fuck me—it's true.

I can't be mad at Langston, at least not for this. *But why does it hurt worse than him threatening to kill me?*

Probably because deep down, I always thought we had a future together. At least as friends. As one time lovers.

But that was always just a dream.

Still, I want to hurt Langston more than I've wanted to torture anyone. I want to strike a hot branding iron into his heart like he did to me with that kiss.

"I'm ready to tell you one truth from the letter in the envelope."

Langston's eyebrows shoot up, and his blue eyes widen.
"Yea?"

I nod and pat the sand next to me, trying to act like I've forgotten all about that kiss. I could fight him, but that wouldn't help. I'd lose. This is the only way to win—with vicious words.

Langston sits down, resting his wrists against the top of his bent knees.

"I want a month for telling you a truth."

"A month seems fair," his words seem pained, hesitant.

"The letter said the first requirement for going after the treasure is to be married. I have to be married. Only that person and I will have the keys to be able to open the treasure. Whoever I choose, I have to choose wisely, because I can only be married once. One love to go after the treasure with."

He looks out at the ocean, his thumbs circling each other, fidgeting. He knows I'm not done.

"Liesel, will—"

"And you can't ask me to marry you to get the treasure. You can't even force me to marry you in exchange for giving me back my life."

"Why not?"

"Because I'm already married to Waylon."

His eyes flash to my hand to see if he somehow missed a wedding ring. He didn't.

"Liesel Dunn wouldn't get married without a gaudy engagement ring."

"Oh, I have a ring. I have everything. We were going to announce it at the next fundraiser event when he announced his candidacy, make a big splash."

"You're lying."

"Am I?"

Langston studies me, but he has no clue. The only way to know for sure is to go look it up in the wedding registry back in New York.

"Yes," he hisses, his pain oozing off of him.

"You can get me to spill all of the information on my half of that letter, but it won't matter. You can't go after the treasure for yourself. This whole exercise in kidnapping me and threatening my life was all for nothing."

Boom.

An explosion rings through my ears.

Langston tackles me to the ground, shielding me with his body.

"What was that?"

"We're under attack," Langston says, but he's not worried. His voice is calm. Fighting a battle is his happy place.

"You have to do exactly what I say if you want to survive, you hear me?"

I nod, my body trembling from his weight pressed against mine.

"I wasn't going to ask you to marry me, that was never the plan."

"Wasn't it?" I breathe, not sure why we are still talking about this when bombs are going off in the distance, growing closer with each moment.

"I couldn't even if I wanted to. I'm married, too."

No.

My mouth falls, my eyes swell with threatening tears, and my heart slows.

"I'm married. I have two kids."

More burning words. He just lit me on fire and left me to burn.

"Your marriage won't help you. You have to be married to a Dunn to be able to go after the fortune, and last I checked you didn't marry me. I'm the only Dunn left."

Langston is quiet a minute.

Another explosion goes off, and somehow his body presses harder against mine until I swear I feel his erection at my stomach. I must be dreaming, though.

"I married a Dunn."

I frown, completely confused.

"You cheated on your wife with me and Phoenix?'

"Phoenix is my wife—Phoenix Dunn."

I search my brain, trying to figure out how she's related to me.

"My cousin," I say, remembering long ago when my father once mentioned I had a cousin. He told me she's the only family I have left if I wanted to search for her. I never did. I didn't want family.

Another explosion, this one close to the house.

"You promise to do what I say?" Langston asks.

I know he won't let me up unless I do.

I nod.

He frowns, knowing I'm lying.

"Run, Liesel. Run until you can't run anymore. Tomorrow, come find me, huntress. Come find me, and I'll tell you a piece from my half of the letter. I'll give you another piece of the puzzle."

Langston removes his body from mine.

I run.

And run.

I run from the pain.

I run from Langston.

I run for my life.

He wants me to hunt for him tomorrow, to find him.

The only thing I plan on hunting for is a way off this island. There was once a time when I thought Langston was the one. The man I would marry—the love of my life.

But this isn't a love story. This is the story of all the reasons Langston and I can't be together.

Reason number one: we lie.

———

Thank you so much for reading Vicious Lies! Langston & Liesel's story continues in Desperate Lies!

Make sure you've read Lies We Share: A Prologue to read Langston and Liesel's past.

JOIN ELLA's NEWSLETTER & NEVER MISS A SALE OR NEW RELEASE → ellamiles.com/freebooks

Love swag boxes & signed books?
SHOP MY STORE → store.ellamiles.com

ALSO BY ELLA MILES

LIES SERIES:

Lies We Share: A Prologue

Vicious Lies
Desperate Lies
Fated Lies
Cruel Lies
Dangerous Lies
Endless Lies

SINFUL TRUTHS:

Sinful Truth #1
Twisted Vow #2
Reckless Fall #3
Tangled Promise #4
Fallen Love #5
Broken Anchor #6

TRUTH OR LIES:

Taken by Lies #1
Betrayed by Truths #2

Trapped by Lies #3

Stolen by Truths #4

Possessed by Lies #5

Consumed by Truths #6

DIRTY SERIES:

Dirty Obsession

Dirty Addiction

Dirty Revenge

Dirty: The Complete Series

ALIGNED SERIES:

Aligned: Volume 1 (Free Series Starter)

Aligned: Volume 2

Aligned: Volume 3

Aligned: Volume 4

Aligned: The Complete Series Boxset

UNFORGIVABLE SERIES:

Heart of a Thief

Heart of a Liar

Heart of a Prick

Unforgivable: The Complete Series Boxset

ABOUT THE AUTHOR

Ella Miles writes steamy romance, including everything from dark suspense romance that will leave you on the edge of your seat to contemporary romance that will leave you laughing out loud or crying. Most importantly, she wants you to feel everything her characters feel as you read.

Ella is currently living her own happily ever after near the Rocky Mountains with her high school sweetheart husband. Her heart is also taken by her goofy five year old black lab who is scared of everything, including her own shadow.

Ella is a USA Today Bestselling Author & Top 50 Bestselling Author.

Stalk Ella at:
www.ellamiles.com
ella@ellamiles.com